Underrated

Morwenna Blackwood

" A thrilling read about urban decay, and a fine portrait of its psychological consequences." **Guy Mankowski, Author of "Dead Rock Stars"**

Novel also by the author:

The (D)Evolution of Us
Glasshouse
Skin and Bone

Cover Your Tracks

To Terry Cooper, in memorandum.

Acknowledgements (original from first edition)

As ever, my first thanks go to my family for all their support while I've been on this writing adventure. And thanks to the darkstroke community – you guys are amazing! Massive thanks also to Lee Dickinson, editor extraordinaire – and yes, sometimes football does get in the way! Thanks to Jenny Kane and PJ Reed - my Costa writing buddies - and to the staff of Costa in Tiverton, where much of this novel was written. Thanks to Ed Hogg for filling in the details of Third Division press-boxes as he remembers it from the 1990s, and also for letting me tag along to all those away matches when I was in my early teens! Thanks to Will Lesser, and Rhiana Orchard for your input about student life at Liverpool University - especially Will for some inspirational anecdotes! Thanks also to Steve Weekes who won the competition I ran during the launch of my previous novel, Glasshouse, to name a character – I gave the parameters, and he came up with 'James Theodore Court: Court being not quite Kirk'. Belated thanks – with apologies! - to Eleanor Graham, my great friend from Uni, who gave me information about the behaviour of blood in water, which I used in my first novel, The (D)Evolution of Us – in the excitement of releasing my debut novel, I forgot to give you a mention! Thanks also to Guy Mankowski and William F Aicher for kindly reading an early version for me, and for their gracious comments. Finally, thanks to Annie Beddow, my college tutor when I was sixteen – if you hadn't used the phrase 'inextricably linked', these novels would not be as they are – thank you!

About the Author

When Morwenna Blackwood was six years old, she got told off for filling a school exercise book with a seemingly endless story, when she should have been listening to the teacher/eating her tea/colouring with her friends. The story was about a frog. It never did end; and Morwenna never looked back.

Born and raised in Devon, Morwenna suffered from severe OCD and depression, and spent her childhood and teens in libraries. She travelled about for a decade before returning to the West Country. She now has an MA in Creative Writing, and has written several novels, short stories, and a collection of poetry. When she is not writing, she works for an animal rescue charity, or can be found down by the sea.

She often thinks about that frog.

Underrated

Will

It's like tinnitus.

The silence with Mum and Dad in the front room is deafening and all-encompassing. Dad's pretending to read the Sunday paper, and Mum's pretending to read the magazine that came with it. I'm scanning the free paper for cheap, second-hand cars, but the pressure in the room renders me incapable of it, so instead I stare out of the patio doors at a load of crows that are hopping about on the lawn. There's that phrase: *you could have cut the tension with a knife.* In all honesty, I wish one of them would cut the other with a knife – or me, or, better still, darling Dominic – because then it would be over with. The atmosphere in here is so tense that it's given me a blinding headache. I stand, deciding to retreat up to my cave, and the sudden movement makes the crows take flight. I wish I could just fly away. Why the fuck do we all go on with this charade?! I can feel myself going mental; at some point I'll crack and then I'll take things into my own hands and force a change. Because this is absurd. It's pathetic. It's fucking killing me!

My bedroom – I think of it as my cave – is small; a dark box with a north-facing window. Even though I'm the oldest, I got last pick – or rather no pick – of the bedrooms, but mine does have a built-in wardrobe, so that, apparently, makes everything all right. Anyway, this room is all I've got, so it's my refuge.

Though I want to slam it, I close my door quietly. It doesn't matter how loud I am – no one notices me, so I don't bother any more. I stare out of my bedroom window onto what is probably the most uninspiring view known to man: the length of our parquet-paved cul-de-sac, with its widely spaced four-bedroom houses and their uniform lawns that run flat from the house to the kerb. All the front gardens sport the designer slash that the housing developers refer to as 'landscaping', which is basically a strip of clay soil planted with hardy shrubs and a rowan sapling that wears a wire mesh dress. Outside every door are generic pansies and lobelia in pots, in varying states of health. And then there's the big, posh house – the former show home – at the open end of the cul-de-sac, blocking out the rolling hills and anything else that might be behind it, except the main road that connects our estate to everything and everywhere else in this shitty little town, which is basically nothing and nowhere.

I can hear my younger sister, Sally, in the kitchen; her overbright voice chirping on about biscuits and essays, while she makes another fucking cup of tea. I want to scream at her to stop it! I grab the nearest sheet of plain A3 – I draw a lot, there's stuff everywhere – and shove it up against the window. I can see the silhouette of the big house through the paper, and I sketch out its rooms as I imagine them, and I fill them with stick figures. I draw a couple fucking doggy-style in the master bedroom, a woman shooting up in the en-suite bathroom, a man stabbing everyone in the kitchen, and a kid with a noose round its neck, jerking and swinging from the landing banisters. I smile and feel better. Maybe my brother should try art therapy.

A new shadow passes through my picture and distracts me. Speak of the devil! I pull the paper down and see Dom stumbling round the corner and into the close, like the Grim fucking Reaper, but with a spliff instead of a scythe, his ridiculous, attention-seeking vampire cloak sweeping blackness over everything. That Metallica song they're always putting on the jukebox in The Riverboat plays in my head – Dom's the *creeping death* of this family.

I'm so fucking angry that my parents seem to turn a blind eye to his shit, but then, what else would they do? I mean, special Dom – the youngest of us all – they're hanging on to their baby, aren't they, even though he's old enough to legally shag someone now. He wants to do art foundation at college, like I did. Why can't he get his own fucking life?! To be fair, his drawings are good, I'll admit that, even though they look like they've been done when he was tripping on acid, which probably isn't far from the truth. They're psychedelic. Like his crappy, trippy dance music. Trance, or whatever. He may dress like a goth, but I know he takes God knows what and dances his ass off down The Tube with the rest of them on a Saturday night. But that's okay, apparently, because 'he's only just sixteen, he's experimenting, he's an Artist '(you can hear Mum give the word a capital 'A'; but if you ask me, 'piss artist 'would be more like it) and – this is the best one – he's 'ill'.

He's got a diagnosis. He's 'mentally ill', whatever the fuck that means! Oh, poor, poor little Dominic with his demons and his tablets! We've all got to 'support 'him, apparently, which basically means let him do whatever he likes. All he's got to do is stop drinking and taking all those other drugs that don't come with a prescription, and he'll be able to think more clearly! He just needs to grow up and take some fucking responsibility for himself. And this is a small town, for fuck's sake – everyone knows who he is and what he does! But he's got – and I quote – charisma. People get drawn in by him. Yeah, he's better looking than me – I know that, and it doesn't bother me in the slightest. But because he dresses like a goth with that bloody Dracula cloak, and stomps about in those red DMs, everyone thinks he's cool. Me and Sally just stumble about in his shadow, picking up the pieces. He's got big-fish-small-pond syndrome, if you ask me.

And it's a bloody stagnant pond, too. I can't wait to get out of this place. When I was his age, I had a job to go alongside my studies, but darling Dom? No, of course not. That would 'stifle his creativity', according to Mum. I could scream, because the irony is, *I'm* the artist! *I'm* the one with the actual qualification in graphic design! Graphic design makes money. It's hard work that gets you into a position to be able to support yourself – not poncing about throwing paint at walls, playing the tortured soul!

Graphic design serves a purpose. It's actually useful in the modern world, and because it's useful, people pay you to do it. If Dom thinks he's going to be able to support himself by selling those pictures, he's going to get a nasty shock. But then maybe that's the point. Dom will never have to support himself, because Mum and Dad will always look after him, while he swans about doing whatever he wants. If he thinks he'll spend his days – sorry, nights; he's a fucking vampire, apparently - churning out these pictures that someone will magically duplicate and package for free, and then sell them to these 'alternative 'wankers who will come out of nowhere, desperate to buy them – then he's more deluded than the doctor thinks.

"You only get one life," he says, as if he's a fucking philosopher or something, "so you need to do what you love." He doesn't think about the fact that you have to eat and keep a roof over your head, and make sure your family is okay. He's selfish as fuck: a dreamer, a waster, a self-obsessed pretty boy. He's just walked over the corner of number one's lawn because there's no fence. Social rules don't apply to him, apparently. Or maybe it's this simple – maybe he just doesn't give a shit.

I've tried my best to get my folks to talk about things, but they just can't see that Dom is the problem. Sally is okay. She's started her A-levels, and she's pretty sensible, but Mum and Dad don't really care about her, either. They just argue and stress about Dom. We've all heard Dom talking to himself, or whoever he says he talks to. Mum says it's just how his artistic side manifests itself; Dad says, well, fuck all, really – he just buries his head in his marking and lesson planning. Or he'll say that Dom just needs to 'cheer up a bit', that he's just a moody teenager, and all this depression stuff is a load of bullshit, like 'yuppie flu'. I'm actually with him there. Dom just needs to get a grip.

Thinking about it, so do I. I'm over eighteen now – an adult! Old enough to legally buy alcohol; old enough to live on my own. I wasn't lucky enough to be able to fuck off to university, but I have a full-time job – I reckon I'd be able to rent somewhere. I can't live in this box anymore, hiding from arguments, painting over cracks. I could send some money to Mum and Dad out of my wages each week, maybe go round on Sunday for a roast, just to keep an eye on everything. Yeah, I'll get a flat somewhere – there are those big houses on the Avenue that they've converted into maisonettes to rent. In fact, I'm going to look in the property section of *The Gazette* when it comes out tomorrow. And someone at work said there are some flats going in Thomas Street. I'm not a fan of Farefield as an area, but it's cheap, and The Riverboat's only round the corner – it'd save me the cab fare home. But I'd be skint.

I run my hands over my hair and face in exasperation, and I can feel another bloody zit on my forehead. I thought my skin would have sorted itself out by now. I pick up my little mirror – well, it used to be my aunt's – and flip it so I can see myself in extreme close-up. The spot is scarlet, with sulphur-yellow pus. I squeeze it, and the pus pops out and splats against the mirror. Disgusting, but it gets the job done. I wipe it off with my sleeve, and everything looks better. When I pull my hair down over it, no one will ever know it was there.

Alex

"Finally! They've employed a decent human being!"

I step back out of the canteen before they've seen me, because I want to see what Elle says to the girl from advertising. I need to know she likes me.

"D'ya mean Alex? Yeah, I'm with you there! I know he's a bit green, and compared to the other lads in the office he's pretty soft. But he's sound, you know?" That's Elle, and she thinks I'm sound!

"Yeah, but he also brightens the place up a bit, doesn't he? D'ya know what I mean?"

"Yeah, he's a good laugh – down to earth, not like all the other bigshot career junkies."

"Elle! You know what I mean: he's fit!"

"Fuck's sake! All right! Alex is a natural – he's brilliant journalist – and yeah, he's fit! Long and short of it is, I would! I definitely would!"

There's no way I can go in the canteen and pretend I didn't hear that, so I pop out of the office for a cigarette. I'll get some food later. But oh my God, Elle is amazing! I knew she had something to do with me landing this job! A job on a daily, in city that doesn't sleep, instead of a local rag in some backwater shithole! I love her! Well, not like that, but I do love her for it. And I won't be the first person to have sex to stay in a relationship. Time to bite the bullet – I'm going for it big time!

October 1994.

Will

I did it. I took a week off work and moved out. Mum and Dad weren't happy. They argued that I could save loads of money by staying at home with them until I had enough for a mortgage at least. To be fair, they were right – they've never charged me rent, even though I wanted to give them some, and on the day I moved my car-load of stuff a few miles down the road, I gave them the grand I'd saved up for them. It didn't go down as I planned. They looked more hurt than anything. What do they want from me?! I can't seem to do anything right! And, yes, I only had a carload. My flat came fully furnished, so I didn't have to worry about any of that. When I got there and the landlord handed me the keys, he said, "Mate, the flat above's going if you know anyone who's interested. And I thought you ought to know – this is a short-term let because I'm trying to sell the building."

Well thanks a fucking bunch.

It was supposed to be the biggest, most happy day of my life so far, and the bastard ruined it by telling me he's trying to sell the building. Fuck's sake. I let myself in and walked around, switching all the lights on. Aside from the front room, the place was dark as fuck. I chucked my rucksack on the sofa and let the door slam on my way out. The one good thing about the day was that The Riverboat was less than a hundred yards up the road. Welcome to Thomas Street.

I'd never been the first one in a pub before. The church clock was clanging eleven o 'clock as I got there, but I didn't take any notice of it until I pulled the door and realised it was still locked. I stood on the step and rolled a cigarette – a nice fat one – and as the main entrance gave hardly any shelter, I stood in the alcove bit in front of the big black gates and smoked it as I would have done any

Saturday night. I wasn't there long before the alchies began to gather. I felt a bit awkward, because this was clearly a morning ritual for them, and they presumed I was joining them. I didn't want to make small talk with a bunch of wasters, so I just smiled and moved over a bit, but one of them – a thin bloke in dirty jeans – slurred, yellow-faced, "Mate, don't suppose I could cadge a bit of weed off you, could I?"

I was a bit taken aback, and replied, "Sorry, mate, I don't touch the stuff."

He just smirked and said, "I may look a bit gone in the head, mate, but I wasn't born yesterday – your coat stinks of it." He had me there, and that's when it started.

Summer 1998.

Will

I seem to spend my entire life scraping Kayleigh up off the concrete, all puke in her hair, the hems of her long skirts all torn and muddy, crying about some bloke, or that her mum left her, or that she's scared about her best mate, Cath, or that she's got no money, or that there's no god and no goddess either … bloody hell, we've all got our own shit to deal with, but we don't have to make a song and dance about it! Or maybe if you have a diagnosis, it's okay. Maybe that's part of the 'healing'. But I still do it. I love her. Fuck's sake.

I know that every Saturday around half nine, she'll burst into the back bar of The Riverboat, singing her head off to whatever's playing, and hugging everyone. Then she'll push her way through to the front of the bar; somehow that bangle-encrusted arm of hers just melts everyone else out of the way so she can slide herself in. And then she'll get served within two seconds. It's like she has an aura, a life-force around her that can't be ignored. You can't see her and not smile – but then she always has Cath in tow. They're like that pair of theatre masks. It's like Kayleigh floats around in a cloud of rainbows, while Cath trudges along behind, flapping at the ever-present flock of invisible bats or rats or ravens or whatever it is she carries round her head with her. And Kayleigh will chat to anyone, everyone, and they'll be laughing, and she'll be blowing her cigarette smoke straight up into the air, so it won't get in their faces, and she'll be dancing to Reef's *Put Your Hands On* and swigging Hooch from the bottle, and it's like she's literally the life and soul of the party every Saturday night … until this switch flips inside her, and I'll be the one picking her up, walking her home, sitting with her in a phone box, talking till dawn on Sunday, and she'll stop crying and sometimes we'll hug and sometimes we'll kiss, and then she'll forget about me till next Saturday night, unless I come into the shop where she works, but I have a drawer full of joss sticks and dream-catchers, and I think her boss, Drucilla or whatever she calls herself, knows I'm not really into all that – I'm just into Kayleigh. Kayleigh's my heroine. I'm living in that Verve song, *The Drugs Don't Work*. In fact, I'm living in *Urban Hymns* – it's beautiful, but it's cold and it's tearing my heart to shreds.

And I did it again, last night! We – Tim, Adam and me and everyone – were on the mushroom stools round the round table, in The Riverboat, drinking, chatting, smoking, eyeing people up, plotting the next pick-up, and Kayleigh came over and plonked herself down on my lap, and interrupted. She downed the rest of Adam's WKD while he rolled a cigarette. Everyone laughed, and we were all flirting. I asked where Cath was – I was quite glad she wasn't there, dragging everyone down – and Kayleigh glanced at Adam and said, "She's in hospital," left it at that, and started banging on about something else, and making everyone laugh, and all I could think of was that she was sitting on my lap, and she smelled of joss sticks and patchouli (under the cigarette smoke and cider) and her mad hair was tickling my face, and I could see the vein in her neck pulsing, and I had to really fight with myself to not just suck it, and I had to go to the loo and bang one out just to get rid of the lump in my trousers – it only took a couple of minutes – then later I picked her up when she was walking home and took her to the party.

Kayleigh had made a show about asking me if I was safe to drive, but I knew she didn't give a shit about drink-driving. She was all about getting lost in the moment. In fact, I think that was her trouble. She used to go wholeheartedly with whatever she was feeling in any given moment. And that's why she broke my heart again and again and again. She was like coke – I knew it was fucking me up, making me paranoid, making me selfish, and that it wasn't helping with my work. Art is a habit, not a personality quirk – but I couldn't stay away from it, and I had to get more, and I had to have all of it, not just a little bit, not just a social thing. The whole routine around it – tapping it out onto a mirror or, more often than not, a CD case, making the lines with my bank card, sometimes fat, sometimes long. Sometimes I had a game with myself, seeing how long a line I could snort. Stuart knew I was caning more than I was selling. I knew it every time I paid for a drink at the bar. He'd clock that the fiver wasn't really flattened out – that it was trying to roll around on itself. Once he even smiled, took it from me, pulled it flat by pulling both thumbs out from the middle, and then licking them. And then I was having to sell it cheaper to him, to pay for his silence, although we pretended with each other that it was just mates 'rates. Fucker. But in the end, he became quite useful, because he was always behind the bar, so everyone knew him, and he could take a break to collect empties and deal that way. A *'have you finished with that, mate?'*, a smile and an upright, matey handclasp passed it over; notes under notes paid for more than just the pint. The perfect set-up. But I'd been talking about Kayleigh.

She'd been walking home – she was living with her mum then, and it was miles away – after the pub kicked out, on her own, stomping along in her Doc Martens, the wind blowing her long skirt, so it kept getting tangled round her legs. I'd parked in the pub car park because there were no spaces in the roads by my flat when I'd got home from work, and it was easy for me just to get in and head off down the 396, across Exeter, and down to Swansburne for the drop, and then on to the party. But I saw her, and I asked her if she wanted to go to the party, and we went to the drop together. I let myself trust her. But then she always goes with what feels right in the moment, doesn't she? It's not her fault. And at least you know she's never bullshitting you. And she could sit in the car while I picked up the package, and then we'd have a nice lot of coke for the party.

"Where is this party anyway?" Kayleigh asked, grabbing my baccy and Rizlas off the front seat as she got in.

"Umm, well it's out in a barn out Seven Crosses way, but I need to go somewhere first."

"Oooh, that sounds mysterious," Kayleigh said, giggling. She started to roll a cigarette. "Ooops, sorry! Force of habit!" she said with a grimace, holding the rollie in her hand like she'd been caught nicking sweets from the Busy Bee.

I just laughed, secretly pleased she made herself at home in my car – it was almost like she was my girlfriend. "Don't worry about it – just roll one for me, too!" I paused – fuck it. "You can always lace them with a bit of something if you like," I said, nodding to the glove compartment. Her eyes flashed, and she popped it open, then looked at me, perplexed by the mess of tapes, maps and cloths. I laughed again, "Check in the box with the spare light bulb."

"What? What do you need a light bulb for in a car?!"

"Oh, one of my brake lights keeps going," I muttered. I love my car and was embarrassed to have to admit that it was actually a piece of shit.

"Shouldn't you take it to a garage or something?" she asked, still rummaging around in my crap. A box of condoms fell out. She held them up, eyebrows raised. Fuck. I could feel myself blushing.

"Bloody hell, Kayleigh, it's only a light bulb; I can do that myself!" I immediately berated myself for my tone, but she just said, "Oh, can you? I thought it was only mechanics that are allowed to do car stuff."

I couldn't help myself – I laughed. "So, if you get a paper cut, do you go to hospital for them to put a plaster on?!"

"All right, fuck off," she laughed. "It's just cars, that's all."

I had no idea what she was on about. But then she was pretty wasted. "You're weird," I said, before I could stop myself.

"I'm weird?!" Kayleigh laughed. "You're the one with a bag of – what is that, speed? – hidden in a light bulb box!"

"It's coke, actually. Dab a bit when you've rolled up."

Kayleigh's eyes flashed again, and we both knew it was going to be an interesting night.

I parked the car on Marine Parade, put my jean jacket on even though it was a balmy evening, and started up the hill towards the railway bridge. "Where are we going?" Kayleigh's eyes were well-dilated. She was buzzing. I put my arm round her and squeezed her close to me, and she laughed and tightened her arm around my waist.

"Shell Cove," I said, "or Horse Cove – I can never remember which it is. Apparently, people get it mixed up all the time." An HST whooshed out of the tunnel and under the bridge, which shook as we crossed it. "Even the railway photographers."

"Fuck!" Kayleigh giggled, grabbing the bridge's iron bars. Then, "Oh my God, you can see for miles up here!" She was right. The sea was flat as a millpond and shimmered a silvery blue-black. We could see the little town, and over the estuary to " –That must be Exmouth over there!" Waves lapped against the sea wall and over the stones and sand of the cove in front of us. "Surely we're not doing it there?" Kayleigh said. "It's right in front of everyone walking along the sea wall!"

"No, not at that one – Horse Cove is the second next along," I said, leading her past the dilapidated block of public toilets, a mess of old canoes and fishing boats, and past the rough red rock that naturally marked the little cove from our destination, Cardinal's Cove. "Anyway, who's going to be walking along a sea wall in the dark?" The only light there filtered down from the streetlights in the park above, but the moon made it easy for us. We passed a line of faded beach huts, and Kayleigh almost tripped off the shallow step. I caught her and said, "Enjoy your trip?" and she laughed, and we walked down the huge concrete ramp and onto the coarse red sand.

"There's no one here," Kayleigh stated.

"Well, they're not going to be standing in the middle of the beach shouting 'Get your coke here!', are they?!" The tide was far enough out for us to be able to see where the breakwater met the sand; as we approached it, it loomed above us in silent testimony to the power of the sea. I led the way across the cove, keeping within the shade of the cliffs. Kayleigh jumped as a train sounded its horn and rushed into the tunnel and out onto the semi-circular wall above us, before disappearing into yet another tunnel.

"Fucking hell, Will," she said, "this is scary!" I laughed and held her tighter as we crunched over a bank of pebbles and reached the dripping cliff face on the far side of the cove. "There's still no one here."

I flashed my eyes at her and started scrambling up the slimy stone breakwater that jutted into the sea to give the railway a bit of protection. If it hadn't been for all the winkles encrusted on the wall, I never would have climbed it in Converse boots. "What the fuck?" Kayleigh said. "I'm never going to get up there in this skirt!"

"You don't have to." I pulled the canoe out of its hiding place, secured to a jagged bit of rock just on the other side of the wall. It made me nervous, the boat being on the other side of the wall all the time. At some point, the lifeboat crews or the police were going to notice it and wonder what it was doing there. But this was the best thing the Scousers could think of after that bloke had his fingers cut off. I tried to shake the thought and dragged the canoe over the wall and onto the sand. Kayleigh just looked at me. I set it in the shallow water and got in. "You'll have to breathe in," I said, as she made to get in the space behind me. "I usually put the stuff in that seat."

"Fuck me, Will; isn't this a bit dangerous?"

"Yes, but until they legalise Class As, it's the only way." I pushed at the sand with the oar, and we bobbed out into the water. The sea was glass-flat, like I said, but I knew that currents can be dangerous wherever you are, so I hugged the rocks.

"It's a full moon tonight, Will," Kayleigh said, her tone foreboding, and almost scared. Without the slapping of my oars, and the lapping of the water on the sand and rock behind us, the night would have been completely still and silent. I held the oars up, and we drifted for a bit. It felt romantic, but that might have been the coke, and I didn't want to spoil the moment, so I said nothing, just watched a slow smile creep across Kayleigh's face. My imagination told me she was thinking along the same lines as I was, and I smiled back and leaned closer.

"What's that hotel called on the moor?" she said.

I couldn't hide my irritation and disappointment. "What bloody hotel and which moor?" I snapped.

Wrapped up in her own train of thoughts, Kayleigh didn't sense there was anything amiss – or if she did, she didn't show it. "You know, that famous one in the book. Dartmoor, I think. Cath's got it on the top shelf of her bookcase with all her favourites, so it must be pretty good."

I was rowing again, and really putting my back into it. "Fucking hell, Kayleigh! I haven't got time to read books! And I hardly even know Cath – she's your best friend, not mine! And she's got a million books, hasn't she? She's going to university to be a writer, or whatever – how the hell should I know?!" I poured all the sarcasm I could muster into that last bit. Another fucked-up waster, like Dom, who the government was chucking our taxes at so they could follow their arty-farty dream.

"All right! Keep your hair on!" Kayleigh snapped back. "It's just it's about smuggling in the olden days when they used to bring a boat into a secret cove in the middle of the night and do their dodgy deals. Actually, are you sure you mean Shell Cove?" I glared at her. "All right, Horse Cove, whatever! Because on the other side of Tamehaven, there's this beach called Smuggler's Cove, and you have to get to it through a long, dark tunnel and down a load of steps that are cut right into the cliffs and there's no other way of getting to it than by sea – shouldn't we be there?"

My anger dissipated, and I couldn't help but laugh – she was so naïve and dippy sometimes, I couldn't help but love her. It was fucking frustrating. "Yeah, right, because no Narc would ever think of looking for smugglers at Smuggler's Cove!"

"Hiding in plain sight?"

She had a point.

Also, I had questioned the fact that these drops now involved a boat trip. Before, it had always been meeting people in the far corners of motorway service station car parks; maybe the police were expecting that now? Or maybe whoever was running this business had done too much Charlie himself and gone off his rocker – that seemed the more likely reason. But the point was moot – this is how we were doing it now, and at least it meant that no one had to even see anyone else, so no one on either side could give anyone away. The canoe stopped moving – we had hit the sand.

Shell Cove – Horse Cove, whatever – is one of my favourite places. Or it had been until those rich fuckers started building their ruddy great mansion on top of the cliff. I love it because you can only get to it on foot about once a year when the tide conditions are right. Otherwise, it's a boat trip, but if you stay close to the shoreline, the people in the big house won't possibly be able see you, and if it's dark, they won't be able to see a thing. They won't live in it when it's built, anyway – it'll be another holiday home. They're just more rich city tossers who think they can come down here and build all over the 'picturesque' countryside they came down to enjoy, then let the building stand empty for most of the year when there are people who actually live down here and can't afford to buy their own home, and then they'll come down for a 'mini-break', drink loads of wine, get their speedboats out, and then fuck off when they've disturbed the dolphins and the seals and the sea birds. Not that I'm bitter. But anyway, we'll have the last laugh, because after a few more years of holes in the ozone layer, the waves will batter the cliff and the whole house will go crumbling into the sea from whence we all came.

Kayleigh hitched up her long, floaty skirt, and tried to tuck it into itself, but there was too much material, and the hem ended up dragging in the sea anyway. She was wearing Doc Martens as usual, so her feet would stay dry; mine, in my canvas Converse boots, were soaked through. I usually took them off and put them in the back seat, but Kayleigh was sitting there, so I didn't, but I don't regret it because at least my feet wouldn't get all cut up on the sharp sand and rocks. Kayleigh skipped up behind me and grabbed my hand. "Where are we going?" She looked around, but there wasn't not much to see because the cove is tiny – a semicircle of sand, surrounded on the curved edge by jagged red cliffs, with the sea wall we rowed around jutting about a hundred yards out into the water.

"Behind the waterfall," I said, smiling at her, holding her gaze. Her eyes flashed again, and I pulled her towards the cliffs to where water continually drips down a naturally formed algae drainpipe, and splashes into a sandy puddle. It's hardly a waterfall, but Kayleigh went all doe-eyed and rushed under it, where she stood letting the cold, salty water soak her clothes and plaster her wild hair flat to her head. She laughed, and her eyes blazed, so I ran under and joined her, and then – finally – we kissed. Soon she was lying beneath me on the sand with the front of her skirt pushed up as high as it could go, and I hardly noticed the icy drops of water hitting my back, and we came at the same time, and it was such a perfect moment, that I kissed her again and again, and told her I love her. She just laughed. Then I lay next to her, and we were silent, smiling at each other. Her hair smelled like salt and vinegar crisps. She looked so beautiful.

I must have dozed off for a bit, because then Kayleigh was shaking my arm, leaning half over me where I lay, spent and sandy, saying, "Will, I think the tide's turning – we'd better get out of here!"

She was right, and I scrambled up, ran through the waterfall and into the sort of cave behind it, climbed up the left-hand side a bit, and forced my cold, wet hand into the leather glove that somehow managed to stay in my back pocket, and reached deep into a hole. The hole was so high up that I couldn't see what I was doing. I wore the glove so that I didn't get all cut up. It protected my hand but made feeling around for the package quite difficult. In the end, I made my hand into a one of those grabbers that you use at the seaside arcades to try to win your girlfriend a toy, and randomly made grabbing movements, hoping that I'd get hold of something. I had as much success as I do with those arcade games, but just as my arm was aching so badly that it was all I could do to keep it above my head, I got hold of the package. It was hard to haul out – it was big – but when I did, I turned triumphantly to Kayleigh. But she wasn't there. She was standing in the shallows, staring out to sea.

We'd both been too lost in the moment to even think about contraception or AIDS or anything. I know Kayleigh shagged around. She just gets caught up in things – she's not a slag. She's free, she's *different,* she's incredible, and I love her.

After that night at Horse Cove, we did a load of coke back in my flat. I wondered if she could sell some through people at the hippy shop where she works, but I didn't want to bring it up in case she thought that was all I wanted her for. And I didn't want to spoil the moment. We sat on my bed, cross-legged, talking and smoking and swigging vodka from a bottle we'd picked up from somewhere. We were literally caning the cocaine, but I didn't care. I wanted this buzz to last forever. I wanted the night to last forever. I wanted to be with Kayleigh forever. I wanted to do that scene from *The Velvet Underground* – was that what it was called? Something like that – I'm shit with films and books – where they snort coke off each other, so I just asked her, and she pulled up her top and I made a long line between her boobs, snorted most of it as slowly as I could, then licked my finger and dabbed a bit on her clit. It was a fantasy come true.

At some point, we put my *South Park* DVDs on and crashed, watching them, and in the morning, I woke up with my arm slung over her waist, and I told her again I loved her. I thought if I said it when I was sober, she'd know I was telling the truth, and she'd reciprocate. I saw her cheeks go up, so I knew she was smiling, but she just said, "I know," and pulled my hand up to her mouth and kissed it.

She needed to move out of her parents 'place, so I spoke to my landlord, and she moved into the flat above me. Then, when the bloke was about to sell the whole building, I did a deal with him and got the freehold. You scratch my back, I'll scratch yours.

And the next thing I know, Kayleigh's pregnant. She didn't tell me – I just watched her putting on weight, and noticed she wasn't smoking or getting pissed any more. One time, I passed her on the bridge – she was heading into town, I was heading home – and there was no one else around. She made like she was going to say *hi* and walk off, so I grabbed her arm. It shocked her, and she whipped her arm away. I apologised, but I was desperate, so I said "Kayleigh – seriously, we need to talk. Look, are you okay? And … fuck it … is the baby mine?"

She blinked back tears that came quickly and easily, and just said, "No, Will. I'm sorry. I'm sorry, but I have to go." And she kind of waddled off up the hill. I thought about running after her, but what would have been the point?

Under the stinging rejection was the gut feeling that something wasn't quite right.

Alex

"Put the fucking phone down, Elle! You're shitfaced!"

Elle glares at me, but she doesn't stop talking. I snatch the phone from her hand and slam it back down in its slot. I expect her to be angry and claw at me with her Shirley Manson-red nails, but she just laughs. She's manic.

"Alex! What the fuck?! I'm so not!"

"You're gurning! Look at you! Your lips are bleeding, and you can't even feel it, can you?!"

Looking me straight in the eyes, Elle licks her lips to remove the blood, but her lipstick is so thick it doesn't make much of a difference. Then, hyper-aware of her movements, she comes over all sensual and tries to wind herself around me like a boa constrictor, but I push her away. "You've got work tomorrow!"

"I know. So let's make the most of tonight, eh?" She's too close to me again, holding me by the hips.

"No! Elle, look, this is getting out of hand. You're permanently coked up – you were just gabbling on to a fucking car insurance company! Fuck knows what they must have thought!"

"I was just being friendly!"

"You were chatting shit! You told the guy you'd be his best mate if he put down that you parked your car in a private garage every night! We're in a fucking penthouse in the middle of Liverpool! Fuck's sake!" I slump on to our cream leather sofa. My mum always said that money can't buy you happiness.

"But –"

"One day, I'm going to fucking record you when you're on one and play it back to you so you can hear yourself."

"What the fuck, Alex?!" Her tone changes in a millisecond. "You've been recording me?"

"No, I said I ought to, so that –"

"Oh my God! There's no smoke without fire, is there? How long have you been doing that? And what else have you been doing?!" Her eyes go as dark as her Dolce and Gabbana little black dress. She frightens me when she gets like this.

"No, Elle. You've got it wrong. All I'm saying is –"

"And all I'm saying is *fuck off*, Alex!" She's grabbed her bag and slammed the door before I can say, "You're fucking paranoid, Elle! You need to get some help!"

Tim

I took the job on *The Gazette* as soon as I left school. I'd done work experience there for a week in Year 11 and enjoyed it, got on with the lads in the office and the girls in advertising. So when one of the juniors got fired for going on a bender, cutting a barge loose and trying to sail it Sampford Peverell because the driver of the taxi he'd hailed refused to drive him because he was too pissed, I applied for the job, even though I didn't have a journalism degree. I must have charmed the editor or something – unless she knew my dad from school – because within a week I had a job as a trainee. I even covered the story about the junior and the barge – Dad thought it was a bit of a slap in the face for the poor bloke, but the guys in the office said I had balls and thought it was funny, so I went with it. Personally, I didn't give a fuck – it's a personal choice to mess your life up, and I refuse to take prisoners.

One day I came into the office to find that the sports guy, Betsy, had gone off sick, so there was no one to cover the match that Saturday. It was a pre-season friendly between Eskwich Town and Exeter City. It happened pretty much every year, and there was usually a good vibe at the Mead because all the Eskwich supporters got the coach to London if City – who were actually in the Football League – got into the playoffs; and as Exeter was only sixteen miles up the road, pretty much everyone knew each other. Also, the Mead was small, and you were allowed to drink beer, so it was always good for a laugh. I grew up watching Eskwich on Saturday afternoons. I stood up, and everyone in the office turned to look at me.

"I'll cover it."

The bloke covering the match for the Exeter papers is lanky, curly-haired, and is clearly a seasoned journo, even though he can't be more than five years older than me. He clocks the press pass I've clipped to the pocket of my shirt, and swaggers over.

"Don't tell me – Betsy went on a bender last night!"

I laugh. I like this guy already. "Yeah, something like that," I say, smiling, rolling my eyes. 'Betsy 'is actually Steve LaBete, a stocky, blond gym bunny who's forever lifting weights and sinking beer and loves the fact that his name means 'The Beast 'in French. Because of this, everyone calls him 'Betsy'. It never fails to wind him up.

"Well hi, Tim. I'm Alex." The curly-haired guy goes to shake hands, and when we do, he covers my hand with both of his own. "Ever done a sports report before, or …?"

"Nah, mate. I'm just filling in. But I'd like to get into it," I reply. Damned right I'd like to get into it – it comes with a pay rise, and you get to go freelance if you want.

Alex is nodding. "Yeah, sports reporting is definitely worth getting into – if you're up to it! It's not for everyone, I'm telling you now, but I enjoy it. It generally comes with more money, and your bylines get noticed. I'll show you the ropes if you like."

"That'd be great, thank you!" I say, giving him a wide smile, which hides the relief I'm feeling.

Alex walks around the edge of the pitch, so I follow him. I'm surprised that no one seems to mind; in fact, everyone we pass gives us a friendly and respectful nod.

"There's no press box here, so we get to sit in the stands with our notebooks, but they generally give us a free pint at half-time to make up for it!" Alex says, when I draw level with him. "It's not so bad now, but it's fucking brass monkeys in winter," he continues, walking over to the old, loud geezer who sells the programmes in the stands. I bet he's been doing this since he was at school. He stinks of cigars and his beer belly pokes out from under his yellow and black replica shirt.

"Oh, I don't need a programme, mate," I tell Alex. "I know most of these guys from school!" It's true. I went for trials myself once – everyone did – but I didn't make the team. The shame and embarrassment crushed me for years but, now I have my press pass, I can hold my head high with them again. Fuckers.

"Yeah, but what about the Exeter lads? And the subs? And do you know the ref's name or how many times these guys have played each other in the past, or if any of the Exeter lads used to play for Eskwich when they were kids?" Alex lets all this hang in the air. I buy a programme. I have to make a story out of this, and if I jot the numbers on the back of the shirts, I can put their names in when I come to write it up.

"I generally sit in the bar at half-time, summarise the first half and see if I can spot one of the managers for a quote. After the match, I'll run over to the dugouts – well, not that there are dugouts here, just those school chairs over there," Alex points up the halfway line to the other side of the pitch where a few school chairs are indeed lined up; some with jumpers slug over them, and bottles of water scattered around, "and get a quote from the managers and whoever they decide is man of the match. Then it's back to the bar for a type-up and check, and then you send it over and get a celebratory pint!" Alex is smiling – it's clear he loves the job. He's made it sound so simple, too, but I'm confused.

"You mean you write the story after, then type it, then send it?"

Alex laughs. "Nah, mate. You write it while the match is being played – the nationals want the report sent over within an hour of the match finishing: the papers go to print at ten o'clock!"

Wow. It sounds exciting, but I'm a bit scared. Reading my expression, Alex says, "Don't worry, mate – you'll get the hang of it!" He grins. I grin. I'll run back up to the office and phone my report over, there – Alex has a heavy briefcase containing a portal PC he calls his Tandy, a modem, and a shedload of wires. This is cutting edge. If I do this well, and keep my nose clean, I reckon I've got a shot at Betsy's job.

It's weird in the office when everyone's gone home. It's like you can feel an energy in there, like you're in a bubble and you know that all these stories are happening outside and are waiting for you to uncover them and write them down and make sense of them and share them and let the world know what's important – the calm before the storm, but a brilliant storm. Although the cleaners have been in, the room still stinks of cigarettes – it's stale and heavy, and I can taste it. Plonking my notebook down on my desk, I scrabble around in my in-tray for the number I've been told to call, and once I've found it, I walk over to the 'facilities', as we call them. The 'facilities' comprise a small trestle table next to the mountain of old newspapers we call the 'archive'. On the table is a white plastic kettle that takes ten hours to boil, a bag of eighty corner-shop tea bags, a small jar of corner-shop coffee, a strangely damp and browning bag of sugar, and a tub of something that masquerades as milk, called 'Quick Five Pints'. Sounds disgusting, but it's actually not that bad – kind of creamy in a strong coffee –

and anyway, there's no fridge. There's a cacophony – I can't think of a better word – of mugs, several stained teaspoons, and a tin of Family Circle biscuits.

Realising I haven't had my tea, I wolf down a couple of jammy dodgers while the kettle has an epileptic fit, and stare at the pinboard. Someone's put a new poster up.

The only thing I have any time for, other than work and *Star Trek*, is music. I haven't been to a gig in a while, but I've heard Thurman on the *Evening Session*, and I know my sister, Cath, likes them – she likes anything indie. Actually, I think Cath said that she and Kayleigh were going. I check the dat. It's tonight! I could go, too. I could do an impromptu report on it for the Entertainment section! Yes! That's what I'm going to do. I tear the poster free of its pins. There're a couple of support bands: Dub Star, and Charcot. Is it pronounced 'Char-cot 'or is it French, 'Shar-coe'? Better find out before I go in – I don't want to look like a twat! But first, my football report.

I wish the cleaners would wipe the telephone wires. Honestly, my once cream-coloured telephone is grimy and greasy with nicotine and smoke, but I can't stop twiddling the coils round my fingers while I'm dictating. Nerves, I suppose. And then, it's done. I've just sent my first sports report off! Bylines, here I come! I'm ecstatic and fancy celebrating with a beer. I'll be off to The Coal Mine to see the band, then!

A quick squizz at the clock and I jog down to the bus station. I shudder when I see the old duck in the wellies in the queue – the whole bus is going to stink of shit until she gets off at Silverton. When we arrive in Exeter, I spritz myself with *CK One,* just in case.

The club is a hole, in every sense of the word. But the atmosphere is intense, and I see the appeal. The bass reverberates through your feet, so your teeth are almost chattering, and everyone and everything is dripping with sweat and cheap snakebite. I grab a pint – it's going for a quid, so I guess they must be about to clean the lines. That, or the lager's off. I stand as far back as I can, on the side next to the sound and lighting guys and put my plastic pint glass on an amplifier. It's not till I pick it up again to take a swig that I see the amp bears the legend, *THIS IS NOT A BEER TABLE*. It is now. Everyone on the dance floor is jumping, and I see Cath and Kayleigh in the centre. Cath looks like she's on E, or something – there's only one word for her expression: bliss. Kayleigh's headbanging, and everyone around her keeps having to pick her tangly, sweaty hair out of their drinks, but no one seems to mind. The band make a final crash, and a skinny guy in a lumber shirt comes on stage and says that Charcot are on next. 'Shar-coe'. I knew it was French! Brilliant!

Betsy turns up at the office the next day. It's gone eleven o'clock, and he's pissed or stoned – probably both – pretending he's neither. He comes up behind my chair and pats my shoulder. "Thanks for covering the match, mate," he slurs, now using my shoulder as a support. "I hear you did a good job. Maybe I'll train you up. Trish, what do you reckon?"

He's smiling at Trish, who slowly and deliberately lifts her eyes from her monitor, and glares at him. I can feel him swaying on my shoulder. He belches. His breath is foul. Trish pulls a heavy glass ashtray towards her and crushes her cigarette out. Betsy urges a couple of times, then throws his guts up all over the blue gingham carpet. Vile, stinking liquid splashes up my chair, over my shoes, and I feel a warm, wet slop on the leg of my trousers.

"Oh, mate, I'm so sorry," he says, his face pale and sweating. "I haven't pulled a whitey in ages!" He starts laughing; the only funny thing about the situation is that his expression tells me he expects me to be laughing, too. Trish stands up. Betsy thinks it's all over. It is now.

After a couple of months of doing home matches, I offer to do away fixtures, too. I say I'll do it at my own expense, when in fact I'm cadging a lift with Alex. He's become like my mentor or something – he's always looking out for me, giving me tips, and I'm really grateful. We both used to watch City when we were younger, and he thinks that Terry Cooper was a fucking legend, too. But then he did take City up in 1990. I suppose we were just into it at the right time. The glory days.

I do wonder why he's helping me so much, though, considering we've just met. No one has ever helped me before. Well, I suppose Trish did by taking me on at *The Gazette*, and Mum and Dad are always giving me lifts and helping me out that way … maybe I'm being paranoid. And Alex is a really nice bloke, too. We went out for a drink the other day after the match, and he told me he loves being a journalist because he finds people fascinating – he's always got his eyes and ears open for an interesting story. He said all he needs is a big scoop that he can sell to the nationals, and then he'll be financially stable and then he can relax. He grinned after he'd said it, but I could tell he was only half joking. It was so great to speak to a kindred spirit; I didn't want it to end. This is all really weird. But I'm rolling with it – this is my ticket out.

Alex

I thought Elle was different. And I thought our relationship was different. I thought she got it, without us having to say anything. Not like a marriage of convenience – not that we're married – but just a partnership that works for both parties.

After she walked out on me, she kept working. She just ignored me. Actually, it was worse than that – she acted like she'd always acted with me, like we'd never been anything more than colleagues. I got to wondering if I'd dreamed our whole engagement. She didn't come home for four weeks. I got up and went to work every day. I even did freelance sports reports at the weekends. I kept food in the fridge, I paid the bills, I put petrol in my car, I did my job, I smiled and joked with the rest of them.

I did all of that, and she saw me doing all of that.

And then one day, she came back. We happened to be leaving the office at the same time for once, and she said to her crew of bigshots and the guys from advertising, "Sorry, lads and lasses, I'm going home tonight," and she got in step with me, we walked to my car, and we went home like nothing had happened.

Except it had happened. She was thin as fuck, she'd almost bled us dry, and I knew she'd been fucking other people. Probably to pay for her habit. I'd read it in the papers and seen it on the news, but I hadn't believed it until it happened to us. Addicts can spend a few grand a week on coke. And I can see the attraction – when your life is falling apart and you're just going through the motions, it gets you out – it makes you feel invincible. And she works so hard – maybe this is what keeps her going. But she needs money to buy the coke, and she needs the coke to escape the pressure of work, but she thrives on the pressure, and she loves the pumped-up feeling coke gives her. It's more than a self-fulfilling prophecy – it's all part of the same thing. She's successful and independent in some ways, but a fucking loser and totally dependent in another.

And she's playing a dangerous game, and if I don't do something, it'll fucking kill her.

Tim

Alex and I are blasting up the M5 with Guns N 'Roses blaring. It's brilliant. He's got a boom box or something in the boot of his car and the piano on *November Rain* is just beautiful. Maybe I need to spend some of the wedge I'm getting from this on a decent sound system for my room. I mention this to Alex, and he says maybe I need to spend it on upfront rent for a flat. He's right. I need to cut the apron strings, and Cath is getting weirder and weirder. Fuck knows what she's doing to her bedroom – she won't let anyone in – but I hear all this scrabbling around on the walls. It's almost like she's writing on them. Somehow, she's managed to get another boyfriend, though – Richard - so the crying has abated a little – mainly because she stays over at his a lot. He's got a full-time job and seems like he's got his head screwed on, anyway. Hopefully he'll be good for her and pull her out of whatever phase she's been going through for the last I-don't-know-how-long. Maybe she'll fuck off to university and take all the eggshells we're walking on with her.

Alex drives fast. And I mean really fast. It's exhilarating. I don't know if it's the speed, or the music, or the fact that I am carving out a career for myself, or whether I'm just having a laugh with someone who's actually on my level for the first time, but I feel … excited. We're talking about football and the tables and how good Danny Baker's Five Live show used to be on a Saturday evening before he got sacked, and work and everything, but also music. He loves Guns N 'Roses. I've got a copy of *Use Your Illusion II* on tape somewhere at home, but I'm more … Madchester, Brit

Pop, I suppose. Although after that gig at The Coal Mine back along, I'm a fan of Charcot, too. They were brilliant – quite heavy, doing epic songs with loads of guitar and piano solos; some of it sounded a bit classical, and they even smashed up the drums at the end! I tell Alex all about it.

"Oh my God, you were at The Coal Mine that night?! Fuck, everyone was talking about that gig! I was going to go, but I had to go shopping after the match because I had no food in the house, and when I got home, the office called me in on a breaking story – you know, when those Scousers got arrested for dealing at the Exeter services, and one of them got his fingers cut off – so I missed it!"

"Oh, yeah, I remember that. Trish gave the story to 'The Veteran 'because it was so big. I bloody shot myself in the foot going to that gig because I went partly so I could write a review for the features page." I'd been cursing myself about that for weeks and the memory stung.

Alex laughs. "You need to chill out, man – you can't do everything at once! And anyway, you covered a legendary gig! You *saw* a legendary gig! Did you contact any of the music mags afterwards? They were hailing it as Charcot's breakthrough gig – it'll go down in history! Did you have a camera with you?"

I kick myself again. "No – it didn't even cross my mind! They would have loved that story! Fuck!" I've got to think like a journalist all the time – get professional. I'm missing opportunities all over the place!

We're about to join the M6, and the traffic is fucking chaos. It's been chucking it down with rain all morning, so the drive hasn't been easy for Alex. There's so much spray coming off the road that I can't tell if it's actually raining, or whether it's just a lot of surface water. Every time he overtakes a lorry, Alex has to flick his wipers to turbo. Now we're just sitting on the slip road, Alex's wipers screeching now that there's no noise from the tyres on the road. My window has misted up, and we've got the heaters going in the attempt to clear the windscreen, so it's hot. We've tried winding down our windows, but we just get soaked. Through the misty greyness, we can see lines of lorries and vans clogging up the near-side lanes, and we hear the odd honk of a horn as impatient drivers redundantly try to switch between the lanes. *Use Your Illusion* has gone round a few times, and now we're aware of it, so Alex pops it out of the tape deck so we can listen to the radio for a while. Rozalla's *Everybody's Free* blasts out from Radio One, and we grimace at each other, so Alex slams the tape back in, and we both laugh. His hand brushes my leg as he moves, and then he taps my knee and says, "Tim, you're doing well. You really are. Just take your time." His touch goes through me like an electric shock.

Early Spring 1999.

Will

I know who shot the crow. It's that weirdo who lives in the top flat of the building opposite mine. I've seen him, up in that protruding attic window, with his binoculars. That's why I work in the back room, even though it's dark. He watches Kayleigh, I know he does. I ought to tell the police. I ought to tell the police a lot of things, but if I did, someone would tell them lots of things about me, too, and I can't have that.

I don't know who the bloke is – he hasn't lived there long, and he's not from round here. What is it with all these new people arriving? First that twat, Richard, who's got everyone believing that the sun shines out of his ass, and now this freak. Why anyone would choose to live in this shithole of a town is beyond me. Most of the population were either born here, or ended up here after some disaster. They've built all those new houses – the *Little Boxes on the Hillside* – near to the North Devon Link Road, and the only way I can account for them going up is because it's cheaper to buy a house here than in Exeter, and it's easy to get to Exeter on the M5. But who knows? Who cares? They'll end up disappointed, like the rest of us. It drains you, this place; turns you into something you had no intention of ever being. Or maybe that's just life. Anyway, my coffee's gone cold.

Work isn't happening today. I've switched on all the lights, and I've got Crowded House's *Together Alone* playing in the background because that album usually sparks something, but today, nothing. I've just been staring out the window at my garden – the thought of weeding it and tidying it up just seems mammoth and depressing – twiddling my pencil and thinking about Kayleigh and that crow and that vet and that bloke and forgetting about my coffee. Fuck it – I give up.

I throw the pencil on the floor and hear the lead snap inside it. I can't afford to do things like that, I know I can't, but I've got to let off steam somehow. I get up, trudge off to the kitchen and fill the kettle. Other than the sound of the kettle boiling, all is still. It's silent, because Kayleigh – the girl I still love – is not upstairs, thundering about, playing Oasis, laughing with her little boy, or telling him off for throwing her stupid crystals. I go out into the communal hall. It doesn't smell of Kayleigh's joss sticks. I step outside, pull the baccy out of my jeans pocket, and roll a cigarette. The plant pots Kayleigh put either side of the door to brighten the place up are full of cigarette butts now, because she is not here to clear them up. And Kayleigh is not here, because she went fucking mental and I phoned the ambulance and the police, and they came and took her away.

My cigarette is almost gone. I take a final drag and bend down to stub it out in the plant pot, so it can rot slowly with its kin. Then I glance up at the attic window opposite. There's a flicker of light, so I presume the bloke is in there, moving about, but I can't be sure. I bet he was watching last night. I bet that's why he shot the crow. I find myself wishing he'd shot me instead – death is underrated, I'm sure of it. No more pain and struggle and doing your best every day just to have it all thrown back in your face by some hippy bitch who's had someone else's kid. I wish he'd shot me. Shit – what if he'd been trying to shoot me?! No, that's paranoia. I've got to stop smoking so much dope.

Anyway, the crow. I nearly stepped on it when I walked out of the front door for my morning cigarette. It was wet and shiny with blood, and though its eyes were closed, its beak was agape. I'd never paid any attention to a bird's beak before, but this one looked as strong and cruel as a dagger.

It was just your standard crow – not a jackdaw, because they're smaller and have grey heads, and it wasn't a rook because they're the ones that hang around in groups and have white beaks. I know this because Kayleigh told me once, when we'd been having a coffee in my garden ages ago, before any of the shit with Richard started happening; before her best mate, Cath, died. We'd been standing with our mugs at the far end of the garden catching the last of the sun one afternoon. She was into herbs and wondered if I could grow some for her so she could use them for a special tea, or something, and I was telling her about the different conditions they like to grow in, and she was standing there smiling at me like I was a fucking genius or something, and yeah, it made me feel really good, and the sun was warm and there was no wind, and a bird was singing really loudly, warbling away, and it was peaceful, and she was genuinely interested in what I was saying, and I remember her face, all pale and smooth as porcelain against the backdrop of her crazy hair that always reminded me of a bird's nest, or a patch of brambles or something, and I remember her lips were a really hot pink, and I just wanted to kiss her, and she was smiling and asking about vetiver, which I'd never even heard of, and then I blushed because I realised I'd totally lost track of what I'd been saying, and Kayleigh's smile widened and I found myself taking a step closer to her, and I put the hand that wasn't holding the coffee cup forward to touch her hair, and it was surprisingly soft, but I only felt it for a millisecond because there was a terrible squawking and we both turned in the direction of the noise, and she said, "Oh my God, that sparrowhawk's got a blackbird!" I turned round to see this brownish grey bird flapping off in the direction of the park, clutching a bird that was screaming and trying to flap its wings, and it was terrible, and we could hear doomed bird for ages. Kayleigh and I just stood there, aghast. It was like the world had stopped in that moment. I realised there was no longer any birdsong, and that my mug of coffee lay shattered on the crazy paving.

Kayleigh reacted first and was on the floor picking the

biggest pieces out of the splat of beige that had been my coffee. "I've never known anyone have as much milk in their coffee as you do," she laughed. "You're worse than my grandma, and she used to drink Mellow Birds!"

I didn't want to hear about Kayleigh's fucking grandma, or be compared to an old lady, so I said the first thing that popped into my head, "How did you know that was a blackbird and not a crow?" And she told me about how she'd always 'identified 'with birds and that she'd been in the YOC when she was little. She said that ravens were her 'spirit animal – 'she's such a fucking hippy! – and we cleared up the mess together, and Kayleigh wrapped up the shattered remains of my mug in some newspaper so that the bin men didn't cut their hands, and I followed her out the front, to put it in the big bin. I lifted and closed the battered plastic lid, which was still warm from the heat of the day, and I realised that Kayleigh had stopped talking. She was gazing off in the direction of the park. Then, in a small voice, she said, "When I was little, I used to wish I was a bird, so I could just fly away from all this crap. Like, really wish, you know?" Slowly and gently, controlling the blood and adrenalin that was rushing through me again, I stepped closer to her and tilted her head up to meet my eyes. But she was crying.

And even though she wasn't there, and even though she would never know, I remembered Kayleigh – and all her hippy karma and shit – so when I found the bleeding crow, I took it to the vets instead of wringing its neck and dumping it in the bin.

I did it all wrong, apparently, just turning up at the surgery with an unconscious, bloody bird in my hands. Luckily, the vet on duty had been between appointments, so when I shouted *help* through the glass door, she ran out to open it – why anyone thought a round, brass knob would be appropriate for a veterinary surgery waiting room, I don't know – and ushered me straight into a consultation room. It turned out that she wanted to go into wildlife rescue veterinary practice after her stint in small animals was done, and she had a particular interest in crows. Well, she said 'corvids', and I had to ask her what she meant. She said they were exceptionally intelligent creatures. She also said pellet guns ought to be banned, and she couldn't understand why anyone would shoot a crow – or any other living thing for that matter. Then she said that the crow's spine was severed, amongst other things, and that she'd 'give it some pink juice to help it over the Rainbow Bridge'. I told her thanks, but that I wasn't twelve years old. I know it's too late for me to leave a good-looking corpse, but, like I said, death is underrated.

I didn't want to go home, so I stopped on the bridge and stared into the fast-flowing brown river for a bit. The railings were wet and cold, their white paint flaking, the exposed metal rusting in places. I let go of them and wiped my hands on my jeans. It occurred to me that I should wash them after picking up that crow, and I looked at where I'd wiped my hands on my jeans. There was a slight red smear on the right leg. Which gave me an excuse to go for a drink at The Riverboat.

The double black gates that lead to the back bar and the toilet were ajar, so I pushed the gap wider, and saw Tim passing Stuart a spliff.

"Sorry, mate, we're closed!" Stuart laughed. He toked on the joint and held it out to me, gesturing for me to come in, and shut the gates. "I'm running low, man," he muttered, his expression serious and almost panicky, "when's the next drop?"

"When's the next drop?" That said it all. These people weren't my friends. But then I'd never had any friends. All I got were people being nice because they had an ulterior motive for wanting me around. I guessed that had always been the truth – it was the key to human survival as a species, when I thought about it. Altruism was a lie. And to be honest, the only reason I was smiling at those idiots and sharing their spliff was so that I could wash the crowy mess off my hands, get a bit of a free buzz on, and maybe get a sneaky pint and a fry-up, too. And I did need their help. I couldn't shift this much gear by myself. Also, they didn't know it yet, but things were about to go up a gear. I needed them all buttered-up.

Alex

They might have got Curtis Warren off the streets, but people are still killing each other over drugs. The demand's insatiable and there's always going to be some ruthless motherfucker willing to get them from A to B. It's never going to stop. I had to walk round the block three times before I felt together enough to come into the office today – two blokes shot a guy, his wife and their three kids as they were getting in their car to go for a half-term holiday to Blackpool, yesterday morning. In broad daylight! Less than a mile from our flat! The police were telling everyone in the vicinity to stay in their homes. You don't mess around with these crazy fuckers! How the fuck am I going to get Elle to stop?!

Late Spring 1999

Will

I met Kayleigh at The Riverboat, like everyone meets anyone here, when she must have been sixteen or seventeen. It's hard to know how old teenage girls are, and the bar staff use this as an excuse to serve whoever is waving a fiver in front of them. All anyone wants is to make a bit of money and have some fun – it's fair enough. The only downsides are the fights in the streets after the pub kicks out, and the inevitable girl falling and slurring all over the place with mascara running down her cheeks, whining about some bloke who won't shag her, then throwing up in the phone box. There're always at least three, and Kayleigh's best mate, Cath, was always one of them. She'd get in a hell of a state every time, and I knew Cath's death was suicide, even though Kayleigh got it into her head that Richard killed her. Of course, he didn't. But they threw him in Channings Wood regardless, poor bastard. What am I saying?! He is a fucking asshole. He deserves everything he gets.

Anyway, like I said earlier, Kayleigh had needed a place to live, so I let her rent out the flat above me. I say 'rent'. I was such a mug – she was virtually living there for free, her and her kid. I'd like to say that I think Liam is mine, because he could have been, but he's the spit of Adam. Not that I need the hassle of a kid in my life – I do enough running around after Mum and Dad and Dom. Sally doesn't give a shit any more – she's too wrapped up in Academia.

And now Liam's dear daddy Adam is back, and Kayleigh's already forgotten that I exist. I'm lucky if I get a smile, or a *hiya* when we pass in the street. But at least Adam has a job, so the rent's getting paid.

And I've got the 'novel 'Cath was writing before she died – let's face it, it was just her diary with the names changed; how anyone thought she would ever make it as a writer, I don't know. And I've got all of it – the bits the police didn't bother to look for, too.

But there's the party I took Kayleigh to when Cath was in hospital. If Adam is Liam's father, Kayleigh must have shagged him the day before she shagged me, or the day after. Maybe even the same day. Ugh! Why do I let her do this to me?!

Tim

Dad pulls into the 'deliveries only 'layby outside the butchers, forces that lie of a smile onto his face, and says, "Have a good day – don't work too hard!" As he always does, knowing that I will work too hard because it's my ticket out.

The Gazette office is on the top floor of a building that sits in the middle of Bampton Street, in the centre of Eskwich. One side of the building makes a corner, though, because there's a kind of side street that leads to the Conservative Club, the pathetic excuse for theatre that I've not been to since I saw *Lily the Pink*, or whatever it's called, when I was about eight. Dom loves it, though, and he and a bunch of mates are trying to resurrect it – just another load of wannabes – but it's a dump, like the Con Club, like the rest of the town. I have to get out, and a job as a journalist is a good place to start. I know that it's only a local, but once I've made a name for myself here, I can go for a job on a national, or maybe on TV, and then maybe London, Manchester, Birmingham, Liverpool, or Aber-bloody-deen. Like that song I've been hearing on *The Evening Session – Make Yourself,* by an American band called Incubus. It hasn't been released yet, but I'm going to be first in the queue at HMV when it is! A small part of me acknowledges that these words sound like they come out of a the mouth of a wannabe, but I push the voice down – I don't want to be famous: I just want to get away from Eskwich and my so-called mates and my boring parents and my fucked-up psycho of a sister, and going to the pub every night, picking up girls, downing bottles of Newkie Brown, having the odd spliff, and endlessly talking about how everything is shit and I wanted to get out. Oh, and rich. I want to be rich.

Richard

I've been banging on my door so hard and for so long the sides of my fists are bruised black. I have to keep stopping because of the pain, but as soon as I do, the panic returns and I have to start again. This is all I can do, except bash my head against the walls, and I want to do that because this is fucking maddening, but at the same time I know that if I do that – if I kill myself – I'll be known as a murderer and a rapist forever and "I DIDN'T FUCKING KILL HER! I DIDN'T! SHE FUCKING SLIT HER WRISTS! ARE YOU LISTENING TO ME?" I'm shouting and banging again, but I am not the only one shouting and banging.

The grille on the door is wrenched open, and a screw in a shirt so white it dazzles me says, "Give it a rest, A6669CW, or you'll be moved to a Cat A, and believe me, you will not like it there!" He slams it closed again.

This is so typical of my life. Fucking God, or whoever, has it in for me. Everyone has it in for me. And I can't get any lower than this without being dead, like Cath – who I DIDN'T FUCKING KILL, by the way – so now is the time to pull myself out.

We are literally and metaphorically like caged animals, here, although pretty much everyone else here is too thick to realise it. After a few days as a 'fish 'it seems that there are two ways to do your 'bird – 'the easy way, or the hard way – so when I'm not working out in the gym, I'm helping in the laundry and doing it gladly. You have to work here, unless you're old – I guess to alleviate some of the boredom – but I'm the only one who seems to take pleasure in it. And I have a goal: to get into the library. One of the screws said you can do courses, so I'll ask to do palaeontology degree, if there is such a thing – you never know. I'm going to play the good boy and do everything I can. They say you can get time off your sentence for good behaviour, and I'm not nervous, because every other fucker in here is shit-scared of me. So I'll play the game. I just need to kill this crushing hatred in me for the irony: I SHOULDN'T EVEN BE HERE – I DIDN'T FUCKING KILL HER!

Time passes. Slowly. My induction week is long gone. My cell mate is in hospital – nothing to do with me – so I have the place to myself, which means I can finally have a wank. It's quieter here, and I am quiet too, but I make a point of holding my head up, looking everyone in the eye as I pass them, and saying *all right, mate?* The screw laughed when I asked him if I could do a palaeontology degree, so I'm doing a fucking diploma or something, in business instead. They said it might help me get another job in retail when I get out. Who the fuck are they trying to kid? I'll be lucky if anyone employs me when I get out, because I'll have to declare that I've been in prison. But I won't go on the dole – I'll start my own business, be my own boss. I virtually ran that supermarket in Eskwich from the day I arrived!

Actually, who am I trying to kid? I'm not getting out. Manslaughter and rape? No chance. I stare at the blank, grey wall in front of me. When I first got in here, I'd wanted to mark the days off in fives, like they do in films, more for the irony than anything else, but I thought better of it, so it's blank. I don't want posters up either, so the only place I allowed my cellmate to put his up were on the bit of wall by the side of his bed. I had the top bunk, so I couldn't see them unless I was looking for them, which I didn't, because it reminded me of Cath's bedroom in her parents 'house. Cath. If she hadn't slit her wrists, I wouldn't be in here. I'd be up north somewhere, doing my degree, living the life I deserve. And as for Kayleigh, they can't prove it was rape – we'd had sex loads of times before. And after. It was that fucking woman judge taking Kayleigh's side …

I feel the familiar anger rising again, and I slam my fist into the wall. Then,

"Morrell!" There's a screw staring at me. Fuck.

"You've got a visitor."

What? "Yeah, fuck off, boss," I say, trying to put some humour in my tone. I've never had a visitor. All the other blokes are there in their blue shirts, trying to look like they're away on business or something, and they walk past my cell deliberately looking the other way – they know no one ever visits me.

"No, seriously, Morrell. You have a visitor: some hippy dippy girl with a bird's nest for hair. Sort yourself out."

My nan's mantra pops into my head: the Lord moves in mysterious ways.

I sit at the little, green-topped table in my short-sleeved blue shirt and a grey pair of what can only be described as slacks. I exchange nervous smiles and eyebrow raises with the other lucky guys. One of them – a white-collar con called Spencer who's managed to become what passes for a friend – gives me a warm smile, and nods. Part of me wants to see this as condescending and irritating, but I know he's looking out for me and is genuinely pleased that I finally have a visitor. He breaks his gaze from mine at a woman's gasp. This must be his wife, Nikki. In baggy trousers, trainers, and a vest top, she looks like she's in All Saints or something. As she hurries over to him, her boobs almost fall out of her top, and I find myself with a semi-on.

"All right, Rich?"

I drag my eyes away from Spence's wife and stare at the girl standing in front of me, on the other side of the table.

Kayleigh.

I very deliberately drop my gaze from her over-mascaraed eyes to the chair she should be sitting on. She perches on the front edge of it and faffs around with her skirt. Ha! It's the same one she was wearing the day I knocked her out – electric blue with some oversized flower pattern on it. I remember ripping it, but she's clearly had it sewn back together. I wonder what she hopes to achieve by wearing it.

I'm burning to ask her what she wants, why she's here, why the fuck she let me be banged up. Actually, I want to fucking kill her. It occurs to me that this is why they fix the tables and chairs to the floor. But I hold my ground. I'm not going to be the one who breaks the silence.

Kayleigh pushes her hair back from her face, and gets her fingers tangled in it. She starts flapping, and I allow myself a small smile. Which she returns. My foot is jiggling, so I force it to stop. I continue to stare at her. She glances around, clocks the clock, bites her bottom lip, faffs with her skirt a bit more and blurts out,

"I know you didn't kill Cath. I'm sorry."

I feel like I've been shot. I did not expect her to say that. A million thoughts flood my brain. I realise I'm sitting bolt upright now, my arms on the table. I watch my hands extend to grab her wrists …

"No contact, Morrell." One of the screws or guards or whatever barks at me, and I whip my arms off the table. I need to compose myself. I realise my hands have balled into fists.

"Will … found another diary. Cath had been … planning to kill herself … I read it … I saw it there in black and white, I …" Kayleigh stops and lets the tears fall onto her lap "… I was worrying about it for ages, and I don't know what will happen to me, but I can't keep this a secret – it's not fair …"

"You're damned fucking right it isn't fair!" I'm standing up, yelling. I've slammed my fists onto the table.

"MORRELL!" It's the guard again. "Sit the fuck down or you'll be back in your cell!" I know he's being nice to me, giving me a chance here, probably because I've never had a visitor before. Everyone is looking at me. Spencer shoots me a warning stare. But these thoughts are secondary because I'm shouting, "I'M INNOCENT! I TOLD YOU I WAS INNOCENT! TELL HIM, KAYLEIGH! TELL

HIM!"

"I TOLD YOU I DIDN'T FUCKING KILL HER! I TOLD YOU I WAS INNOCENT! YOU CAN'T KEEP ME IN HERE ANY MORE!" My fists are bleeding.

"Morrell! Shut the fuck up!" The nice screw hisses at me through the blue-barred door to my cell, "You have to get a grip on yourself, or they'll do that psych assessment, and then you'll never get out!" This stops me, and I follow his eyes to my fists. The blood is dripping on the floor. I stare the guy full in the face.

"What psych assessment?"

Tim

I can't help but be excited, stomping up to the top of the stand at Spotland, following Alex to the press box. Being in the press box for your local side is one thing, but here, with my laminated press pass clipped to my jacket, I feel like I've arrived. I feel special. I can sense the eyes of the early-in Rochmoor supporters, programme sellers and ground staff heavy with respect for us, as we climb the steps. The press. I am The Press! It doesn't even matter that the press box at Spotland isn't fancy. In fact, Alex says it's almost one of the worst press boxes in the division, because it isn't even a box. It's open to the elemen ts, so coats and gloves are obligatory pretty much all year round, and woe befalls anyone who tears a sheet of paper out of their notepad – Alex has had pieces of story snatched from frozen fingers by the cold north wind and scattered to the crowd more than once. There is a redeeming feature to the Rochmoor press pen, though – the club provides us journos with 'award-winning 'pies at half-time, and my God, are they good?!

We slide, single file, onto the tired, wooden benches that slump sadly behind another piece of wood that separates us from the crowd. There isn't a lot of leg room even for me, so I really feel for Alex, as he tries to crunch his lanky limbs in, get out his notebook and set up his Tandy. I follow his lead and begin to organise a workspace for myself, while greeting the home press and other visitors, keeping up with the journo banter, and trying to look like I've been doing this for years. There's an undercurrent of sarcasm, of being long-suffering, of resignation, and everything smells damp and musty – stale cigarettes and old meat pies. I drop a Biro, bend to retrieve it, and find the floor dusty and dirty with cigarette butts, greying splats of chewing gum, Mars bar wrappers and fossilised pie gribbles. There are no women, and thank God, because everything is an innuendo! It is, apparently, typical of every press box in the division – Alex says the only difference between them is the dialect. I retrieve the pen, brush my hand off on my jeans, and flip through the programme. I'm enjoying myself.

It's the back page that most interests us sports reporters – the team line-ups. It's vital to check them when the announcer reads them out before kick-off. Recognising members of your home team is easy, but although I'm familiar with the names of the Rochmoor players, I know I won't be able to distinguish them once the games is in play – making notes of the numbers on the back of the shirts and correlating them after is all anyone could do. Having said that, the feature pages can often spark a theme or tone for the report, so it's always worth giving them a quick squizz.

There's a deafening screech, and we all jump out of our seats and then laugh at each other. I drop my pen again. The announcer is welcoming everyone to the game and giving out general information – that's all it is – but in true Division Three style, though the sound levels are clearly switched to max, you can hardly make out a bloody word the guy is saying – and his thick Yorkshire accent makes it muddier than ever. I turn to Alex and laugh. He just pops the lid off his Styrofoam cup, raises his eyebrows, and takes a gulp of steaming brown liquid.

The match ends up one all, and the rain exhausts itself into drizzle. Alex, me and the other journos hang around by the players 'entrance when we've drafted up the bulk of our stories, waiting for the manager, Peter Fox, or one of the players to come out and give us a quote about the match – a vital element of any sports report. We chat about the match, where it places us in the tables, and smoke some cigarettes. It's great! I feel like part of something – something important, relevant, current. I love the camaraderie, the banter, but most of all, the delicious smell of liniment that's wafting up from the changing rooms. There's something intoxicating about it.

All too soon there's an eruption of shouting, laughter, and that overpowering liniment smell – the changing room door opens, and Peter appears and walks reluctantly up the players 'tunnel to talk to us. He is immediately mobbed. I can't believe how pushy some of the reporters are! The TV people try to muscle in and take him off for a private interview, their bulky camera equipment and the fluffy, mop-like mic on the long stick – which Alex informs me is called a boom-pole – getting in everyone's way. But Alex stays relaxed with his notebook and Biro, gets in there first with the questions and even manages to make the City manager laugh. Finally, he asks him if he feels disappointed by the team's performance, and whether he thinks this will have an impact on the rest of the season. I remember having watched Terry Cooper – the previous manager, from the days when I used to go to football matches for fun – being asked a similar question, years ago. He'd smiled and spoken the phrase that stayed with me for the rest of my life: *you've just got to get on with it.* Trying so hard to write down every word 'Foxy 'utters, I miss what he's said – I'll have to get it off Alex later – and know I'm going to have to learn shorthand. I can totally understand what he'd had meant when he said that sports reporting isn't for everybody.

Our footsteps make an echoing, hollow sound as we all stomp back up the wooden steps to the press box, and then there is a cacophony of voices exaggeratingly enunciating their reports over heavy black telephones, phones ringing, modems making their high-pitched, two-tone growl, and always the mad tap of fingers on keyboards. And then it's done.

It's dimpsy now ('dimpsy', I need to get that word out of my vocabulary! They say you can take the boy out of the small town, but you can't take the small town out of the boy, but I think bollocks to that – I'll exorcise it if I have to), and I feel that Saturday night rush coming on. I'm naturally high as a kite, in love with this new life, and the fact I've carved it out for myself out of nothing – and I love the tech I'm using, the people I'm meeting, seeing my bylines in the papers. I can't wait until the day Mum and Dad are watching *Grandstand*, and Des Lynam says, "And now we go over to Tim Locke at St James 'Park."

Alex and I make our way back to his car, and I'm looking around me, trying to absorb the moment, take in every detail so I can remember this feeling forever, from the sounds of Saturday night in Rochmoor, the smell of the takeaways, the daisies growing up between the gaps in the kerb stones, the posters on the lamp posts and the windows of boarded-up shops. And that's when I see that Charcot are playing at The Coal Mine in Liverpool tonight. It's the same poster they used for their gig at The Coal Mine in Exeter, except for the venue and date information.

Alex notices it at the same time, and says, "Instead of stopping for a warm, dry fry-up in Knutsford services, why don't we go to the gig?" His eyes flash. I grin.

James

I stand as close as I can to the Liver Building without

looking proper weird and tip my head back. My eyes can't focus properly, but I can make out a turquoise shape right at the top, so I mouth *'iya* to Bella. I'm a bit soft on the Liver birds. They're 300-odd feet up in the air, so they should be able to see everything, but they're chained down because if they met, mated and flew away, Liverpool would cease to exist. Apparently. And they can't even see each other to get any solace because Bella's facing out to the ocean, watching over the seamen, while Bertie's gaze is fixed inland, keeping an eye on the city. They were built in 18-whatever, so I'm surprised that it's not Bella watching over the city, like a mother watching over her brood, while Bertie, the male, goes off doing the dangerous exploring and bread-winning. But then maybe Bertie is like a headmaster, or the army or something, and Bella's like a mermaid who can lure the fishermen back in if they get ideas. I wonder what they say to each other up there. I imagine them to have harsh cries, like the cawing of crows, or something. It's anthropomorphic, I know, but I can't help think that they're in love, and simultaneously bound by their duty, so it's all a heart-rending tragedy. Or like the plot of a Marvel film, or something – super-heroes sacrificing their love lives for a cause that's so much bigger than themselves. But maybe they hate each other, like an old couple who really should have divorced years ago, and now live together, but alone, in bitterness because it's too late for them to do anything else. Maybe they're bored and want to face the other way for a change. Maybe sometimes Bertie goes *I spy with my little eye,* for a laugh, and Bella gets a cob on and says, *shut up, ya gobshite!*

Anyway, thinking of them makes me feel bad for thinking that maybe it wouldn't be so bad if Liverpool didn't exist any more. I just want to get out of here! I turn my back on the birds and walk over to one bank of the Mersey. I lean on the white railings and stare into the brown water. Only Bella gets a sea view from here. All I can see is the wide, muddy slash of the river, and then the east side of the Wirral. The wind's baltic and it blows the strains of *Ferry Across the Mersey* down to me from the port where they take the tourists out for guided tours. That fucking song does my head in.

I kick an empty tinnie into the road in frustration, and head back into town.

I think about the battles over the UCAS forms. I was made up when I got straight As and knew I'd be going to uni. I wanted to go to UCL, Exeter, Durham, Warwick, or at least Manchester, but because I was going to take a year out to travel round Europe and hopefully California, Mum insisted that I go to Liverpool Uni. They wouldn't see me for a year, she said, and if I studied at a university in the south, that would be it – I'd be gone forever. I battled with her. "You're building a holiday home in Swansburne, for God's sake! It couldn't be any closer to Exeter! You could come down and stay there any time!"

"He's got a point, love," Dad admitted. "He could even stay there instead of getting some ropey house share in the city."

"You're missing the point, Dad! I want to get away, meet new people, be somewhere else! I …"

"If you don't take your place at Liverpool University, we will not fund your year out!" Mum dropped the bombshell.

"Fine!" I retorted. "I'll use my own money!"

"And how far do you think your supermarket wages will take you? Hmm, you could get to France, possibly the Balearics, and then …?" Mum paused for effect, her head cocked to the side, and watched me as my dreams of Amsterdam, Rome and San Francisco stepped up to the gallows in my mind. I couldn't let them die.

"Fine," I said, "but I'll never forgive you for this."

And I don't. The arguments between me and Mum get so bad that she's not even surprised when I tell her I've got a room in the Mulberry Court halls of residence. At least it's goodbye to Allerton. I've just got to get on with it. I'll carve out a new start for me somehow.

Tim

Alex wants to stand at the bar and chat, and I do too, but when Charcot come on, there's such an energy in the building that I find myself dumping my pint with a puzzled Alex, and virtually jumping over to the dance floor. And that's when I see him. Floppy blonde hair plastered to his face with sweat, fitted black T-shirt and tight jeans, Reebok Classics, right at the front, clearly off his face and giving it all to the band. At that moment, I understand the meaning of the phrase 'I've had an epiphany – 'I want this guy. Like, really want him. I can feel it, and everything I've been feeling about and worrying about Alex these past few months suddenly becomes crystal clear. Unless it's a phase. Unless it's a response to my crazy mother and my fucked-up sister. I think about my girlfriend, Sally. I glance over to Alex, who is watching me from the space he's carved out at the bar; his eyes fix on mine over the top of his pint. I know I should go back over, or beckon him over, or something, but I can't stop myself. I *need* to speak to this guy. I know that Alex can see it in my eyes, and I know I'll have to try to make amends in the car on the way home – unless he dumps me here and leaves – and that would have a massive effect on my career, and I owe him so much – and I know he can see it in my face – he knows everything, and I can almost feel his heart break, and I can feel the tears welling up and the salt stinging, and in that moment it's like Alex reads my mind. He gives me the smallest of sad smiles. Permission. Acceptance. Like Terry Cooper used to say, you've just got to get on with things, so I push my way through the jumping, rocking, moshing bodies, and cheap cider or lager or snakebite – if they have snakebite up north – spills on me, but I get to the front, and I start jumping in time with this blonde enigma, and he turns to catch my gaze and says – or rather shouts, so he can be heard above the relentless music '" –Iya! I'm James. James T Court – it's not quite Kirk, but it's as near as dammit!'" He laughs, then, "And next time you're at the bar, I'll have whatever you're having! 'Make it so!'" He's a Trekkie!

He's got a mobile and gives me his number when the lights come back on. He's a student. He lives here. He wants to see me again. What the fuck am I going to do about Alex? What the fuck am I going to do about Sally? Why the fuck don't I care?

Richard
"Hello, Will."

I can't stop the smile spreading across my face. I want to laugh. The guy's in shock – he's usually pale, but his skin goes almost translucent. He just stands there with his stupid little arsehole of a mouth open.

"Well, that's not much of a welcome home, is it?" I grin, shove him aside and push my way to through to the bar. "I'll have a pint of Krony, Stuart, when you're ready – and put it on Will's tab, yeah?"

I can feel the fear radiating off everyone, and it's pathetic. What a bunch of losers. What happened in The Riverboat when I walked in is so cliched, it's painful. Sudden hush, and all heads turn my way, like I'm a lion at a watering hole. My release has been all over the news. That twat from *Spotlight,* Katy Has-been, even wanted to do a feature on me, but I told her where to shove it, even though I really needed the money. That's the irony of it: these people are afraid of me when I didn't actually do anything. They're afraid of me even though I'm standing here in a grey tracksuit that could only have come from one place. The screws told me they'd thrown away my clothes when they brought me in; probably couldn't be arsed to clean and dry them when they thought I was going to be banged up forever. Bastards. I should look into getting compensation. Also, I have no job. Who's going to employ an ex-con – even if I have been exonerated? Stuart is, that's who.

"You must be fucking joking!" Stuart spits. I've stayed all day – drinking at the bar, nice and quietly, scouring the papers for a means to live, and somewhere new to live it, watching the pond life of Eskwich dull the razor edge of monotony – and now he's got the bell for last orders in his hand, ringing it like he's metaphorically smashing my face in.

I smile at him. "I assure you, I'm not. You like to think of yourself as a nice, fair-minded guy, don't you, Stuart? I've been cleared of all charges. *I'm* the victim here, although it pains me to admit it." Stuart looks up and down the bar. I don't know where he thinks he's going to find back up. You can't fight the law. You can't change the facts. I've been cleared.

"You want to watch out for women, mate," I continue, draining the last of my pint. And, staring him straight in the face, "They may look all sweetness and light, but every single one of them is trying to screw you for something – case in point: Kayleigh. Yeah, she's pretty, she's a decent shag, but she's a fucking liar."

I let it hang there. Everyone knows Kayleigh was sectioned. The courts, and the NHS, have decided that when she pressed the charges of murder and rape, she was manic. Delusional. And now *she's* the one with the appointment for a psych assessment. Funny how the tables turn. Poor, poor Kayleigh.

I saunter home. Yes, home. I thought I would lose my flat, but then I remembered Nan's inheritance. That bastard woodworm of a brother of mine may have got half of it, but I had enough to pay off the mortgage, and to get them to return my car to its garage. I think the fact that I pursued this helped me – why on earth would I bother paying off my mortgage if I knew I had to spend probably the rest of my life in prison? And in spite of myself, I'm grateful for that, even though my dream of going to university has gone out of the window. Actually, has it?

Someone has scraped the word *cunt* into the black paint of my front door, but other than that, the place is exactly as I left it. I'd expected a brick through the window, or dog shit through my letterbox, but there was nothing. I stumble a bit, going up the stairs – I haven't drunk in ages, and steadily drinking Krony all day hit me in the face as soon as I got out in the air. The maisonette doesn't feel like home, either – everything's in disarray from where I'd chucked stuff in boxes when I 'moved in 'with Kayleigh. Which reminds me – I need to pay her a visit and get my stuff back. I make myself the first decent coffee I've had in a while, spark a Marlboro from the pack I find on the sofa, and lean out of the window. I watch the pissheads staggering home – some teenaged lads singing about how they 'hate Argyll', some tarts arguing with each other about who shagged Barney first, and who he really loved, and a dishevelled bloke with long grey hair and dirty jeans trudging back up into town with a bottle of Newkie Brown in one hand, and a plastic bag in the other. I've got to get out of here. But not yet.

Then I smell it. It's faint, but detectable through the cigarette smoke. Metallic, almost acrid, unmistakable. Blood.

Funny how you seem to not notice things around you until you're away from the usual for a bit, and then when you come back, they slap you in the face. That first pint of Krony hit me like a tonne of bricks. And now I've come back home – home! – I can smell the blood again. Cath's blood. She cut her wrists in my bath. She left me to find her, to deal with all her shit, and to clear up the mess. Selfish bitch. I thought I'd cleared up pretty well. Once the ambulance had taken her away, and Kayleigh had gone, I'd drained the bath water, mopped the floor, and cleaned the bath with Jif. I never realised how sticky blood is. It had all kind of congealed at the bottom of the bath, and I had hell of a time getting rid of it. I'd had to dig my hands in and scrape it off the enamel. It oozed through my fingers and was all under my nails. I picked up great slopping handfuls of it and dumped it on a bin liner I'd laid on the floor.

Selfish fucking bitch! It was all, *poor Cath, how terrible, she must have been so frightened, murdered by her boyfriend, who'd have thought it in sleepy old Eskwich, he seemed like such a nice bloke, but it just goes to show, you can never tell, can you? And her poor family. And poor Kayleigh, losing her best friend, and then having a baby...*

It was poor fucking everyone else, but no one gave a shit about me! They just added four and four and got 1,296! Why are people so keen to believe things that are written down? Like Nan with the Bible. It's a fucking book, for God's sake! And Cath wanted to be a writer – a professional liar! And because of that, not only did I lose my girlfriend, and have to clear up the entire contents of her veins, I ended up in prison! But it does go to show that you should always read a book through till the end. It's just fucking typical that the only one who read Cath's novel through to the end was Will, and he only let on that there was an ending because he got screwed over by some slut as well. Sad twat that he is, still chasing after Kayleigh.

And that releases me from my reverie. I'd moved a load of my stuff round to Kayleigh's. Once the stench of Cath and lies and bitches is out of my house, I'm going round to retrieve it.

James

I think I'm hungover. I have never felt like this after a night out before. It's horrible! I fall out of bed and tumble to the bathroom, where I throw up spectacularly, all over the toilet. I have jelly for legs, my eyes are streaming so I can hardly see, and someone is battering my head with a mallet. When my stomach is empty and I have stopped dry-heaving, I just sort of hang off the toilet seat for a while.

Then laughter bubbles up in me. Laughter at my state, the state of my bathroom, the fact that I don't know how I got home, the fact that I don't know if I am alone, or if I brought someone home, the fact that I don't know where my mobile phone is, that although I feel like utter shite right now, LAST NIGHT WAS BOSS! Oh my gosh, the band, Charcot, were incredible. Honestly, they were insanely talented, and the whole crowd knew it, and the whole crowd was jumping, and I was higher than I've ever felt before, and I fell in love! Yes! Finally! I finally fell in love, and it was love at first sight – just like I knew it would be! I am actually so happy I cry. It's like an epiphany. This feeling is holy. I glance up to the picture of Jean-Luc Picard, that hangs above the toilet, and thank him for making it so. He gives me a Mona Lisa smile.

Adam

That first night Kayleigh, Liam and me spent as a family was incredible. It was bliss. The way I could finally love her now – openly – and look after my child, who even I can see is the spitting image of me, was just overwhelming. Yes, we were in a crappy flat in Farefield, that Kayleigh had filled with crystals and witchy stuff, and it was a bit of a mess, and her mum was there, but we were a family, finally. After everything. Yes, okay, I did feel bad for Will, her landlord, because anyone with half a brain cell could see that he was in love with Kayleigh, but fuck it; in life there are winners and there are losers, and in this instance, Will was the loser. Is a loser. But I didn't dwell on the feelings because I now knew I had Nan's money behind me, so I could support my family, put a deposit down for a mortgage, and get us a house on Moorhayes or Canal Hill, or maybe even get out of Dodge and relocate to Exeter. Also, I didn't have to worry about hiding any more. Cath was gone. I would never find her camped on my doorstep in tears again; I would never have her break into my house again. And it turned out that my brother, Rich, had murdered her, so I don't even have that nagging doubt that she killed herself because I didn't love her any more. I had never felt freer.

It's ironic, I suppose. I'd never felt so free, so the very first thing I did with my new-found freedom, was throw it away by shacking up and trying to play happy families with Kayleigh. What a twat! What was I thinking? Yeah, the kid's lovely when he's not crying – it's nice to hold him close and have him fall asleep in my arms in front of the TV in the evening; it's nice to go out and buy him little toys, sing to him and that. And Kayleigh is amazing. I mean in every kind of way. I've loved her for so long. But the trouble with loving someone for a long time and not being able to be with them, is that you start going into this little fantasy world in your head, where the thought of the person consumes you, and you have little daydreams about them, and the force of your love, and then when you actually get back with the real person – well, it's disappointment. There's no other word for it. Yeah, the sex is great, but the constant getting up in the middle of the night to hush a crying baby is a fucking killer when you have to work every day. I have never been so fucking tired in my life. Kayleigh lets me stay in bed while she sorts it all out, but I'm not deaf, and then she's banging about in the kitchen getting bottles and putting the steriliser on at three in the morning, and then when Liam won't go down, she starts crying and getting upset, and then I have to sort out two blubbery messes while all I'm doing is checking the clock to see if I can get any more kip before my alarm goes off. And I can smell the nappies in the bin, and I can see all the laundry piling up. I mean, she's home all day, for fuck's sake! Why doesn't she just leave him to cry in his cot, and go and sort the house and herself out? No one ever died from crying, did they?! And if she just breastfed him, there'd be no need for the already cramped kitchen sides to be full of bottles and steriliser bits – I mean, fucking hell, it's not like she hasn't got any boobs! Not that I get much to do with them these days, because she says they're sore all the time'…

I am thinking all these things, opening the fridge to get out another Krony, when she flounces in, all jangly earrings and long skirts. Liam is crying in the other room, and her face is like thunder.

"Bloody hell, Adam!" she snaps. "Can't you put some of this stuff away?!"

"Well, it's your flat – I don't know where everything goes!"

"Well, you should do by now!" Kayleigh snatches a bottle, shakes the milk, peels off the foil lid of that bottle, and then pours the milk into the bottle, muttering under her breath.

"Jesus, Kayleigh, what the fuck is wrong with you?!" The words are out of my mouth before I can stop them. "You've been acting funny since you went into Will's house the other day before you met us in the park. What's wrong? I am the father of this baby, aren't I?"

"Of course you are! Don't be such a twat!" she spits, flouncing off. Within seconds, Liam's crying has stopped, but I can hear her dragging in air, muffling her own sobs.

And then, suddenly her mum is left in charge of the baby – her mum, instead of me! – because Kayleigh is going out again. I'd believe her story about doctor appointments, except I saw one of her letters on the kitchen table the other day, saying they needed to see her at that psych unit, The Beeches, again, and she's been offered an appointment for like six months 'time. So where is she off to for the morning?

In all honesty, I am happy that Kayleigh's mum, Sandra, has taken charge with Liam. He's a great kid, but it's weird how I suddenly feel relief when I go off to work. I used to dread those twelve-hour shifts in weaving, but now when I'm there, at least I feel like me. I am in control, I know what I'm doing, I know when my breaks are. I know I'll get banter and laughs, not screaming and crying and the relentless fake smiles and forced happiness of kids 'TV. I can deal with the lads, and the noise and the earplugs and the sweat, and the having to have everything done yesterday, and nothing being good enough for the boss, and the bitter coffee in the canteen, and the lack of windows. It's easier than walking on eggshells around an even-more-up-and-down-than-usual Kayleigh, and willing Liam to sleep, and then wondering if I'm doing enough for him and whether he's developing right, and whether he's getting enough 'tummy-time '(fuck's sake) which he hates, and worrying if we should be taking him to the swimming pool more often, or whether he's getting too much TV because we're tired, and worrying that this flat is a fucking shithole. The one thing I don't worry about now, is money. It's a really strange, but beautiful feeling. At least the rent will be paid, the bills are covered, and we have enough food. And when I go into WHSmith, I can buy the odd album. I've even got some new jeans! And I don't feel like such a skinflint when I'm in the pub, either: I can actually get a round in and not have to worry about what everyone is having. I should be happy. I know I should. I have money, I have a job. I have a family. I finally have Kayleigh, which is all I've wanted for years. Years and years. I had to move away for fuck's sake. And now we're living together, with our son. But I'm not happy. Maybe it's a case of the grass always being greener on the other side. Or is it because I've lost the freedom I didn't know I valued so much? Or is it something to do with Kayleigh?

It's something to do with Kayleigh. I've been on

weekends this month, so Tuesdays and Wednesdays have been my days off, and I've noticed Kayleigh's disappearing every Wednesday afternoon. She says she's got weekly appointments with Dr Whittle, but I'm fucking sure those appointments don't last three hours, so where the fuck is she? I confronted her the other day, and she says she goes up to Cath's grave for a bit afterwards, but that smacks of bullshit. Also, she keeps going off for chats with her mum in the kitchen, and then when I come in to see if anyone's making a coffee, they both jump, and these fake smiles come up, and one of them will say something like, *well, yeah, I'd better get the washing on*, and then one or the other of them will go off. Something's going on. I'm not stupid, for fuck's sake. Will stares daggers at me when I meet him in the hall. I was watching *Babar* with Liam on the sofa the other day – he loves that bloody elephant! – just sitting there with him slumped on my lap, his podgy fingers grasping mine so tightly I could feel his sharp little nails, and I was sort of half watching the show and commenting on it for him, half looking at his hair and his hands, and I was suddenly struck by the fact that his hair is slightly darker, more golden brown than blond, and his fingers look longer, and observing all this, I wondered if he was actually my kid, or whether he was Will's. I know Will's fancied Kayleigh for years, and it wouldn't surprise me if she's shagged him at some point. My rota shifts back so I have weekends off next month, so this Wednesday, I'm going to follow her.

Sandra is happy to look after Liam for the whole afternoon. It's a crisp autumn day, and Liam has been pointing and cooing at the crows flying past our front room window all day, so she's going to take him down by the river to feed the ducks. I smile when she tells me, but I can't suppress the lurch that goes through me whenever I think of Liam around water. He's so fast on his feet now, and hell-bent on wherever he's going. I have visions of Sandra chatting to whoever's walking past, or stroking their dogs or whatever, and little Liam toddling off down the concrete slope to try to pop a bit of bread in a swan's mouth, and splashing and falling in the water, or the swan flapping its wings and breaking his arm, but Kayleigh's mum reacting too late, and then the headlines in *The Gazette* on Tuesday – TODDLER DROWNS WHILE GRANDMOTHER PATS DOG. It doesn't bear thinking about!

Anyway, this is the only chance I'll have for a month, and if Kayleigh is at the hospital and the cemetery, then there's no problem.

Kayleigh is jittery from the moment she wakes. She's up and fussing over Liam immediately, even though he's still asleep. I'm lying there with a semi-on – the thought of following her today has turned me on – and I beg her to come back to bed, but she says she's got a headache and needs a cup of tea and hurries out of the bedroom. She's wearing the oversized T-shirt she got from a gig at The Coal Mine – Thurman. Whatever happened to them? It was the last gig she went to with Cath. Her hair resembles a clump of brambles, and now she's losing the baby weight, her arms and legs are returning to the lithe, toned, sexy shape I fell in love with. My cock surges, and I get out of bed and follow her to the kitchen.

The kettle is boiling, and she's leaning against the worktops, arms splayed, head down. It's absolute chaos – we'd been too tired to do the dishes last night, so in addition to all the baby bottles, the steriliser, the excess food that won't fit in the cupboards, the coffee cups and crisp packets, there are saucepans and plates and cutlery encrusted with dried pasta sauce, and somehow the cheese grater is on the floor amongst the breadcrumbs – the whole place is a state.

I pad up behind Kayleigh and hold her hips. "Adam …" she says. I know she doesn't want this, but the urge in me is so strong, I bury my face in her neck and kiss and tongue it, trying to turn her on. "Adam …" she says again, pushing back from the worktop, craning her neck into my head in an attempt to push it away. My hands have been circling her hips, and now I slide them up under her T-shirt and touch her breasts. She inhales sharply, and groans, and even though she says I know her boobs are hurting, I pinch her nipples, which makes her gasp. "Adam!" Her tone is insistent, so I drag my hands down her stomach. "I've got a headache, for fuck's sake! I'm not in the mood!" She pushes back, attempting to stop me, but the action pulls my hands lower, and I touch between her legs. She's wet.

"Sure you're not in the mood?" I tease, stroking.

"Adam …"

"Come on, Kayleigh, we haven't done it in about a week – I'm dying here!"

Kayleigh sighs, puts her hands back on the worktop, and I slip inside her, still stoking her clit. She slaps my hand away, and snaps, "I'm not going to come, so don't even bother!"

I know I should stop really, but the need in me is so strong and, now I don't have to worry about pleasuring her, I can concentrate on my own orgasm, which comes quickly and with a rare intensity, and I'm still spurting when Liam cries, and Kayleigh drags herself off me to go tend to him. I watch my cum oozing down the cupboard door as I get my breath back.

Sandra takes my place on the sofa beside Liam at eleven o'clock. I've told Kayleigh I'm filling in for four hours for a mate at work. She visibly relaxes when I tell her, although her foot remains jiggling. Instinct makes me look up at our window as I leave the garden, and Kayleigh is there, watching me, with Liam in her arms. I've caught her out – I can see the surprise on her face – and she gives me a stupid little wave. I'm in my Farefield Fabrics top, and I turn right and go round the corner. I'd planned to wait behind the big tree in the church grounds, but now I'm going to have to loiter here until she goes out. Will's Polo is parked on the side street opposite, so I scoot over and crouch behind it, pretending to tie my shoe. Kayleigh usually leaves at quarter past eleven, so I won't have to wait long.

And suddenly, there she is, her long skirt with its tattered hem, billowing out behind her with the wind and the speed of her walk. I have never seen her walk so quickly. As she crosses the road to go past The Riverboat and up the hill, she breaks into a little trot. If she'd been going to the hospital, she would have turned right instead of left when she got out of our yard and onto the street. She would have walked right past me. And even if she'd been buying cigarettes on her way to the hospital, she wouldn't have crossed over and be going up the hill. Bitch! I knew she was lying!

I jog back over the road, hoping without checking that Kayleigh's mum isn't looking out of the window. Kayleigh is halfway across the bridge now, and I have nowhere to hide if she turns around. I will her not to, but it's clear she's hell-bent on a purpose, trotting over the road between the town hall and St George's church. I'm only a few feet behind her when she turns right into Memorial Lane, and jogs down the hill, hair and skirt flapping, clasping her rainbow-patterned canvas bag close to her side to keep everything from falling out. The reverse-warning honks on the 55B bus start up, and Kayleigh runs, waving her arms at the driver, shouting for him to stop. He stops, of course – she's pretty. She stumbles on board, dropping the fiver she's been clutching in her other hand, and all I can think of is *why is she going to Exeter?* And then, *how the hell am I going to follow her?*

I duck behind a bus shelter pillar, facing the wall, again hoping not to be seen, and listen to the bus reverse, go round the roundabout, and head off for the main road to Exeter. I wait there until I think there's no chance Kayleigh could see me, whichever way she's facing. I watch the back of the bus growl out of view. Fuck!

"Trouble in paradise?"

I jump about a foot in the air, and turn to see Will, a smarmy grin oozing across his face, standing so close to me I can smell the skunk and stale booze on his denim jacket.

"I can tell you where she's going, if you ask nicely," he drips. What a prick. Who the fuck does he think he is?!

"Fuck off, Will." It's all I can manage, and I shove past him and start walking back up the hill, my anger increasing my speed. I want to know what Will has to say, but pride forces me away from him and back home. I'm hoping that he'll come after me and blurt out whatever it is he's got to say, but I think I've blown it – the smug wanker will probably slope off to wherever it is he goes, and delight in the fact that he's got one over on me. To be fair, that's what I'd do.

I'm nearly at the top of the hill before I hear Will's feet slapping behind me. I allow him to catch up, and he grabs my shoulder and jerks me to face him.

Will is furious. He's such a loser, I didn't think he was capable of strong emotions – clearly, I was wrong. His eyes are so wide and livid that he almost scares me.

"She's gone to see Richard," he spits. "I'll leave it to her to tell you why."

Tim

We leave the B & B after what would have been a beautiful fry-up if the atmosphere hadn't been so strained. I'm trying to pretend that nothing happened, that I was just pissed up; I'm trying to convince myself that this crushing feeling is just a hangover. Alex is quiet, smiling, but sad. He looks hurt. I swing between terrible waves of guilt, and anger –

what the fuck is going on here?! Alex and I aren't a couple! I haven't cheated on him! I'm not even gay; I have a girlfriend, for fuck's sake! I had fun at a Charcot gig, chatted to other people … okay, I drank a bit too much, but so did Alex! I can't make sense of what is happening … I must be hungover. This is just alcohol paranoia.

I stuff half a sausage into my mouth, and engage Alex in conversation about the Rochmoor match, the amazing pies, how the tannoy could be so loud, but we still could barely understand what the announcer was saying. After a while, Alex relaxes and we talk about City's play-off hopes, and the next away match. I think he has forgiven me, but he's quiet during the drive back. We listen to music, but I suppress the urge to talk about it because I know that if I mention Charcot, the darkness will descend again.

Sally meets me in The Riverboat. She's standing at the bar talking to Stuart when I arrive, and it's so obvious he fancies her, I cringe. He's leaning between the taps, cloth in hand, absentmindedly wiping down the bar, but it looks like he's thinking about wiping down something else. The old alchy with the greasy white hair is flapping a fiver around, but it takes an "Oi! Romeo!" before Stuart jumps to attention and starts pulling the guy's usual pint of Guinness. I stalk over to the bar, sliding my arms around Sally's waist, which startles her, and makes Stuart blush. She's wearing a long, floaty skirt with some fucking gross flower pattern on it, and a vest top under her leather jacket. She's very pretty, but her look is a mismatch – like she can't decide who she is. She kisses me full on the mouth before saying "Hello," and I hope she didn't sense my reluctance to kiss her back.

Stuart brings us both a drink – a Krony for me, and a Hooch for Sally. The lemon scent clashes sickeningly with her White Musk body spray, and I have a Radiohead moment and catch myself mouthing the lyrics to *Creep*.

"So where did you get to last night?" Sally teases, swigging from the green bottle.

"Sorry, babe, I meant to phone after the match, but it was so hectic, and then I saw that Charcot were playing at The Coal Mine in Liverpool, so Alex and I headed over so I could do a gig review – I'm hoping the *NME* will take it."

"Bloody hell, Tim! You were seeing Charcot, while I was sat at home revising, waiting for you to phone and ask me out for a drink! Nice. Thanks for that." Sally's annoyance and sarcasm are short-lived, though, because she proceeds to tell me all about her revision for her psychology A level, nattering on about Pavlov and Skinner, whoever the fuck they are. I feign enthusiasm – what she's saying is interesting, but all I can think about is dialling James 'number. I wonder where he is and what he's doing right now. I down the last third of my pint and tilt the glass at Stuart, who nods acknowledgement from the JD optic. Getting pissed seems like a good idea.

James

This module on developmental biology is fascinating. I'm especially interested in metamorphosis, particularly holometabolas and I've been up since five reading about wasps. I love this! Research kind of turns me on – I feel high, like I'm getting to the answers, like there is so much to learn, so much I don't know, and, crucially, so much I could discover. I was in the uni bar last night, talking to some guy over a watered-down pint in a plastic glass who turned out to be a second-year art student, studying English Lang and Lit, and he told me about a book by some bloke called Kafka – *Metamorphosis* – which I really must buy from Blackwells when it opens later. He was totally bladdered, waxing lyrical about how the physical and the psychological are inextricably linked, and that if I'm studying physical metamorphosis, I ought to take a look at political, psychological and metaphorical metamorphosis, too. I was so intrigued, I bought him a pint to thank him.

It was 'traffic light night', and I wasn't surprised when a goth girl holding a green glass came up to 'Eldritch 'and commented that she loved how he'd done his eyeliner; Eldritch turned away from me, dinked his green glass against hers, saying "Cheers!" and I'd downed what was left in my red glass and made for the door.

I blush at my secret – I'd gone for a red glass, full of the memory of Tim. Silly, sentimental, but it had felt like the only thing I could do. I've got this urge to get the train down to Eskwich – it's near Exeter, apparently – to find him, but I have to give him time. It's been a couple of days now, but I know he'll call me. I hold my Nokia against my chest and will that ridiculous generic ringtone to start up. De-de der der de-de der der de-de der der der. Nothing. I stuff the phone into my pocket and grab my bag – I need to be in the lab in half an hour.

Tim

"Look, Sally, I know Cath's a bit fucked up, and I know you find that fascinating, but it's a fucking nightmare to live with, and she's my sister! Can we talk about something else for five minutes?"

We're at my house, in my room, and we've just had sex really quietly, so my mum and dad didn't hear. I pretended to come when she did, then pretended to be dozing for a bit, so I didn't have to concentrate on her chattering. I always get a bit sleepy after sex, while she gets really energised. It's fucking annoying. And I don't want to think about my sister when I've just had sex. Although I soften the sentence as I end it, Sally puts on her hurt expression, apologises and reaches across the pillow for my hand. I let her take it, although I don't return the squeeze.

"So what do you want to talk about? Did the *NME* take your article?"

"Yeah, they did," I say, my enthusiasm rising, "and

hopefully I can combine away matches with gigs and kind of do a two-in-one. I just need to keep my eyes on the music press. They only gave me twenty-five quid for the review, but twenty-five quid's twenty-five quid, innit?"

Sally smiles and squeezes my hand again. I know what she's thinking – this journalism thing seems to be taking off for me, and I've got some money behind me now. She wants me to move out of my parents 'place and get a flat. She wants us to move in together, but I don't know how much of that is because she loves me, and how much is because she wants to get out of her parents 'house, too. Her youngest brother, Dom, has been sectioned again, and she's always going on about how her mum and dad are at each other's throats.

"There are loads of places going in Farefield," she urges. "Will – you know, my other brother – has got a massive place on Thomas Street, and if he can afford it, I'm sure you can! Imagine us living together – it'd be sick!"

"Sick?! You've been watching too much MTV! Fuck's sake, Sally, you're in the middle of your A levels, I'm all over the place with my work … it's not the right time! And anyway, I don't want to get some crappy flat in Eskwich – the whole idea is to get out of here, and for that I'm going to need some serious money. And we've not even been together that long."

I wish I could take those words back. Sally lets them hang in the air, giving us loads of awkward time to think about subtexts, hidden agendas and Freudian slips. Eventually, she breaks the silence with, "What are you thinking?" I run my hands through my hair. I can't reply. I don't know what to say. Then, in a small voice, she asks, "Are we okay?"

Are we okay? Surely if she has to ask the question, she knows the answer. I want to be gentle with her, tell her it's over, that I'm so sorry, but I think I'm gay, that I'm moving on, that she's a great person and she'll find someone better, that it's not her – it's me. But I don't.

I cringe at the irritation in my voice as I reply, "Yes, of course we are, but take a fucking chill pill! Once you've finished at college, you'll be going to uni, and unless I get one hell of an exclusive story I can sell to the nationals, I need to save up. I mean, eventually, I want to move to London, or Manchester, or Liverpool … somewhere with a pulse. Don't you?"

"Well, yeah, but what's wrong with Exeter? They do a good psychology degree, and we could go to The Coal Mine all the time, and we'd be close to our parents … you could get a job on the *Echo,* and get all the exclusives on City, and maybe I could help Dom and Cath …"

"And we're back at Cath again!" I throw the quilt off me, hurl myself out of bed, and yank on my jeans.

"What are you doing?" Sally is sitting up, and even through my anger, I can see that her eyes are wet.

"Going out!" I snarl, shoving my arms into my T-shirt, then rummaging in my pockets for change.

"But wh …"

"Oh, just fuck off, Sally!" I slam my bedroom door, rush down the stairs and out of the house, and run to the nearest phone box.

I shove a quid into the slot in the grimy, black phone and punch in James 'number. I've never called a mobile from a normal phone – from anywhere, actually – and other than that it will be expensive, I have no idea how much it's going to cost. The phone ticks for ages before it makes the connection – long enough for me to register that someone pissed in here last night. I stare at the prossie's cards stuck up next to the phone. They're all dog-eared and manky, and I imagine the old alchies tearing them off so they can see the numbers better, breathing beer fumes, all hot and noisy, on them. The phone starts to ring. My pulse races. I feel a bit sick. James doesn't pick up immediately. I try not to panic, try not to count the rings, try not to imagine him thinking *just hang up, loser! I was just pissed up! Fuck off!* The ringing stops. I take a deep breath. "Welcome to the Vodaphone voicemail …" A posh lady's voice. Not James. He didn't pick up. I hear the beep, but I'm choked up – I can't leave a message. I slam the handset back into its holder, bite back the tears, wait for my change. None comes. The call has taken it all.

Adam

I watch Will swagger up Memorial Lane, and really have to swallow the urge to run after him and punch that grin off his face. I turn back to the roundabout and stare around, realise my mouth is open and my fists clenched. What am I looking for?! A taxi to pull up, so I can jump in and say *follow that bus!*? I need to get a grip. Richard's in Channings Wood, which is near Bishopsham. Unless she's meeting someone in Exeter who's going to drive her there, the only way she can get there is by train – but am I really going to get a taxi to St Davids, grab Kayleigh on the platform and confront her? Or jump on the train just as it's pulling out, and storm through the carriages looking for her, like I'm James Bond or something? And what am I going to say to her, anyway? Fuck it. I'll bide my time; see what she's like when she comes back – I'm good at that.

Walking back up Memorial Lane, I realise that I can't go home, because Kayleigh's mum thinks I'm at work already. I don't actually start till six. Which gives me a good five hours to kill. There's only one place to go – The Riverboat.

"All right, mate?" Stuart says, pulling me a pint of Krony before I've asked for anything.

"Cheers, mate, but I have to work later," I say, taking the glass from him regardless.

Stuart laughs, "But one won't hurt, right?!"

I just raise my eyebrows at him as I take a swig. It tastes good and I feel better already. "I'll have a fry-up later, mate, if you can do me one – that'll sort me out."

"When's your shift start?"

"Six."

"Yeah, you'll be fine." He laughs and turns his face to another punter, saying, "Yes, mate?"

I sit at the bar and look around. There aren't many in, but it's busier than I thought it would be. I'm in the back bar, but I can hear alchies getting more and more animated and rowdy in the front. It's like the old people have the front bar, with its beige wallpaper and flowery carpet, fake plastic flowers in greasy, dusty vases, faded paintings of country scenes in gilt frames, and the youngsters have the back bar, which is infinitely cooler, and cavernous without the Saturday night hoards. A guy called Stephen painted the entire room like a cave. It's all stonework and painted melting candles in painted craggy alcoves. There's a painted troll leaning up against the fruit machine, smoking a pipe. At the very back, there's a raised bit that operates as a stage where bands play, and a fairy or a witch or whatever the fuck she's supposed to be sits on the back wall, all blue and white and silver, with her crystal ball. There's a little dance floor in front of the stage, and the ceiling in this area of the pub is ridiculously low. It reminds me of The Coal Mine in Exeter a bit. I sit at the round table in front of the bar, facing the back but unable to see the witch, through the gloom. I twist my pint glass on the table, making wet spirals on the wood, and roll a cigarette.

"Just having the one, are you, mate?" Stuart jokes as he pulls me my third pint.

"Shit. Okay, this is the last one. And I'll have that fry-up now, too, when you're ready," I reply, sliding my overfull pint off the bar and slopping it on the dirty wooden floor as I return to my seat.

I expect Stuart to just drop my food in front of me and get back behind the bar, but he plonks himself onto the stool opposite, puts his elbows on the table, and stares at me, intently. He glances behind him, and into the corridor out to the loos and the front bar, before saying under his breath, "You could just carry on, and do a bit of this before you leave – it'll sober you right up." He opens one of his hands just wide enough for me to see a money bag like you get in the Post Office, with a bit of white powder in the bottom.

"What's that? Speed?"

"Nah, mate. Charlie."

"Charlie? Charlie Brown?"

"Nope, just Charlie. Pure as the driven snow. It's fucking A."

"Where'd you get it?"

"Will."

"Will? What, that loser me and Kayleigh rent the flat off?"

"Yeah." Stuart laughs. "Apparently he's been dealing to that band, Charcot," (he pronounces it *char-cott)* "and they've got connections up north. Don't say anything, though – I'm not supposed to know."

"So how do you know?"

"Will went to college with the drummer."

"So?"

"The drummer's a fucking cokehead – he can't keep his mouth shut – and Will'll say anything to make his dick look bigger."

"Well, cheers, man," I say, making to kind of high five him so he can pass me the bag.

"Hang on – it's not fucking free! I could lose my job if anyone sees us. I'll do you mates 'rates this once, but everyone has to pay up."

I finally click. "What, are you dealing in here then?"

"Fuck. Yeah. Under the bar. But this is between you, me and the lamp post, right?"

I nod, stuff the last of the fried egg into my mouth, hand over more notes than I'd like to, and slide the wrap into my jeans pocket.

At half five, I lurch into the cold, stinking toilets and lock myself in a cubical. I grab a bit of bog roll and wipe the top of the cistern. I rack up a nice fat line with my cash card and roll up my last fiver. I've only done coke once before, and I'm kind of excited. I push the fiver inside my nostril a bit, bend over the line of white powder that's speckled with rocks, reach up with my free hand and pull the chain. The noise of the flush hides the sound of me snorting. Once the line's gone, I sniff again, really hard, and shiver as the drug hits my brain. Stuart wasn't lying – this is good stuff. I suppress a laugh, lick my finger, use it to wipe the traces of powder left on the cistern, and dab it on my tongue. I love the tingle, and the way my mouth immediately feels smooth and a bit acidic. I shiver again. Yes, this has sobered me up. Time to go to work.

Tim

"All right, kiddo?" Keith says. "Who took the jam out of your doughnut?"

"Dad's in the front room," I reply, avoiding the question, stepping back from the front door so he can get in. It's Friday night – Dad and Keith's boys 'night, and Keith's turn to drive. They'll go out to the Heron, put the world to rights, drive back into town, get a burger, and sit in our front room stuffing their food and drinking JD and Coke, watching crap TV, until one of them needs to go to bed. Obviously, Keith has seen *Lock Stock*.

"Bloody hell, I feel sorry for you, Steve," I hear Keith mumble as he pushes the door and disappears into the front room, "living with two moody teenagers. Got ya work cut out there!"

"Yeah," Dad returns, "makes you wonder what the hell you did wrong."

"Kids, eh? Who'd have 'em?!"

I sigh loud enough for them to hear, stomp back upstairs,

and slam my bedroom door on the sound of their laughter. Cath is crying again next door. I hear her get off the bed to turn her music up. *Linger,* by The Cranberries. I used to like the song, but now it just makes me uncomfortable. I take the Charcot EP I picked up at the gig in Liverpool from under my pillow, stick it in my midi system, and switch the volume up until I can't hear the jangly guitar from Cath's room. It's great, and I smile at the memory of that night. But almost instantaneously, it reminds me of James. Now Cath and I are both hiding our sobs in guitar music.

I am woken up in the middle of the night by the thought that maybe James didn't recognise the 01884 code I was ringing from. This hopeful thought is immediately dashed by my memory of the fierce intelligence behind James' eyes – it showed through in spite of all the drink and whatever drugs he was on. Of course he knew it was me. And then, what if he'd been busy when I rang and tried to call me back thinking I'd called from my house? He probably thinks I'm ignoring him! I literally jump off my bed, now glad to find I had fallen asleep in my clothes, run down the stairs, out the front door, and all the way to the phone box. I am scared, excited, elated, and I'm clinging to the hope that I'm right so tightly, that I think I can hear it ringing as I approach. The phone isn't ringing. I think there's a number you can dial that tells you the number of the person who called last, but I can't remember what it is, and I don't think it would work in phone boxes anyway. I shove another quid in the slot, convinced James will answer on the first ring. After the eighth ring, I am crying. "Welcome to the Vodaphone voicemail service …" I want to die.

My sister is dead. Cath is dead. She was murdered by the man she was going to marry – Richard. If he lives to be released from prison, I will kill him. I swear to God.

My family is broken. I am broken. I call James every day from the phone box, and sometimes from work, but he never answers. Why doesn't he answer? I work hard. I work long hours, and it helps. It keeps me from dwelling on things, and it keeps me out of the house. I am going to have to move out – I can't bear to see Mum and Dad like this. They are shadows. Everything is black. I want to die, but I can't kill myself – not now Cath's gone. Sally keeps coming round – even rings me at work – but I refuse to see her. I know she thinks she's still in love with me, but I know she'll want to know all about Cath, and then about me and how I am coping, so she can use it in her thesis, or whatever the fuck they do at university. She can't help it – she's driven, like me. I think that was what kept me in the relationship for so long. That and the fact I was pretending to be straight. Alex and I still go to away matches together, and often to a pub after. We've talked a lot – even kissed once – but he knows as well as I do that we're never going to be in a relationship. I'm just hanging on. We're all just holding on. And I'm spending more and more time in The Riverboat. It's such a cliché. Heartbroken journo seeking answers – or oblivion – at the bottom of a pint glass. The trouble is, I seem to need more and more to get me pissed each time I go in. It's like my brain can't relax enough to let me get para. I need something else.

James

"Cheer up, JT! It could be worse – you could come back as a Glanville Fritillary!" Louise smiles at me. She's my lab partner today, and I like working with her because when she smiles at me, it's literally just a smile – there's no sexual subtext. And she's as interested in holometabolas as I am, although her fascination with wasps is bordering on unhealthy.

"Go on, then," I laugh, "what's so bad about being a butterfly?"

"Ha! It's not the adults – they're the lucky ones! Not enough meat on them, you see. The *Hyposoter horticola* female stalks the butterfly until it lays its eggs, then stakes out the clutch. When it sees the tiny caterpillar about to hatch, she goes in and lays her own eggs into it. The larva waits until the caterpillar is almost fully grown and devours its entire body, then it spins its own tough cocoon and emerges as a wasp! And some species paralyse their hosts and eat their way out of its body while it watches! It's incredible!

"They are so good at what they do! And they're important pollinators. And they keep the bugs off our crops. I can't understand why everyone hates them! Massively underrated as a species. At the end of the world, it'll be wasps, gulls, rats and humans. And possibly cats. Opportunists. I wish I could be that bloody-minded. You know, fuck everything and everyone and do what you're driven to do without any care for anyone else."

"Sounds a bit extremist, a bit psychopathic, no, what's the word … sociopathic, Lou!"

"Yeah, I know, but think how much you could get done! It'd be boss! If I didn't have to worry about what our tutors think, what my parents think, whether I'm keeping that sad cow in the room next to me awake, about remembering my nan's birthday … all that stuff … I reckon I could have found the cure for cancer by now!"

"Yeah, but if you did all that, what would be the purpose of finding the cure for cancer?"

"Therein lies the paradox of the human condition. Makes you wish you could be a wasp, really, doesn't it!" We both laugh because, as ever, the discussion has come full circle. Everything comes full circle eventually.

I do know what she means, though – I'm finding it harder and harder to concentrate on my work, because I can't get Tim out of my head. I don't know what's wrong with me. I saw him that one evening, and he's completely taken over my life. Just that look when he had to go. It's a cliché, but it was like time stood still, even though it passed too quickly. It was painful for both of us to break eye contact. He was moving away, keeping his eyes on mine for as long as physically possible, trying to say everything in a stare, and we were aware of the people shouting and drinking and sweating around us, the ringing in our ears now the music had stopped, the stickiness of the floor, the plastic pint glass splintering under Tim's foot as he stepped back, the gravity of the tall bloke he came in with pulling him away from me when all he wanted to do was stay. He was staring into my soul, ripping it apart, and I gave him my number. I can't believe he hasn't called! Why hasn't he called?

Maybe it's because I told him my name was James T Court. *James T Court – not quite 'Kirk', but as near as dammit, haha!* Why couldn't I just have said, *hi, I'm James?* I hate myself sometimes.

He probably thought, *Yeah, he's fit, but he's such a loser.* If he even thought that.

Will

As Tim slips into a state that's more unconsciousness than sleep, the bottle of Diamond White he's been holding falls onto its side. The dregs spill and soak into the dry earth. I don't know how anyone can drink that shit – it smells almost sulphuric. Still, I catch myself making a grab for it, but the summer breeze pushes it out of my reach, over the bank, and into the water. I could get up, walk down the slope and get it – the water's hardly deep enough to cover my boots – but I can't be bothered. I spark up a Marlboro and watch the bottle as it twists a bit in the current. It might make it to the sea; it might get caught in the brambles. I decide that if it makes it out of my sight, I'll hop in the car and drive down to Exmouth, or, better, the Warren, and sit on the sand with a pair of binoculars and look out for it. How long would it take? I could wait – I literally have nothing to do and nowhere to be now. The current seems to be pulling it out into the middle of the river. I wonder if I have enough petrol to make it all the way down there. I wonder how many bugs will get trapped inside it on the way. I wonder if a killer whale will swallow it and die horribly. Ha! It's got stuck on the sandbank – well, stone bank, really. I expect Tim will go down and get it and see if there's anything left in it when he wakes up. I give his Reebok Classics a kick. Nothing – he'll be out for ages. The clock chimes seven times. I'll get some chips on my way to the pub.

James

My student loan pays for my return ticket from Liverpool Lime Street to Exeter St Davids, and the bus from Exeter to Eskwich. Every single person in my carriage gets up at some point, and weaves down the aisle, holding on to the tops of the seats, trying not to knock out the orange reservation tickets slotted into almost all of them, and makes their way to the buffet car, where they buy mini bottles of wine, or grossly overpriced sandwiches, or both. I'm brassic – I can't even afford a bottle of water, and I'm so thirsty by the time I get to Birmingham, I'm considering swigging from the tap in the train toilet. I don't though, and as I'm wobbling back through the *Krypton Factor* of luggage, long legs and shiny shoes, and cuff-linked arms holding broadsheet newspapers, I spot an unopened bottle of Coke on a fold-down table – its owner must have got up to go to the loo or something – and I do something I've never done before: I nick it. I just swipe it up, carry on down the carriage, flop back down into my seat and crack it open.

A clock is chiming seven when I get off the stinking bus in Eskwich. I climb the hill with purpose, but when I get to the top, I realise I don't know where Tim lives, or what pub he drinks at, so I wander aimlessly about the streets like a fucking tourist. I'm starving, and I spot a bench on some grass by a kind of ford and sit there with my head in my hands wondering what the fuck I'm doing. In despair, I look about me. It's pretty – a double-arched low stone bridge, mallards, shallow, clear water, ancient horse chestnut tree – and then I see him. Tim. I've run over to him before I've realised what I'm doing. He's on his back, sparko. He stinks of cheap cider, and he's covered in puke. When I wipe the vomit from his lips, I can see they've tinged blue. I roll him onto his side, praying he's not already dead.

The hospital is a small, squat building that reminds me of a scientific cell figure. All the departments coming off a central hexagon. I can't believe it's this small. Devon is literally proper west. On the train coming down, the rolling fields seemed to go on forever, like a vast green splat at the end of the country, like an ink blot, but when I got to the centre of Exeter, everything was tiny. The buildings in particular. It's like the architects down here don't want to outdo the hills. And the hills themselves are pretty half-arsed. Just bumps in the landscape, really. Exeter is the capital of the West Country, or so Mum said when they were planning the house on the cliff in Swansburne. Or maybe they're right – it's grim up north, with the cities constructed like monstrous glass shards stabbing the grey sky. The question is, which does Tim prefer?

They wheel him away from me, probably wondering who the hell I am and what I've got to do with Tim's condition. And what do I do? I've taken his wallet and found his ID, so I know his address. I'm duty bound to get in a taxi and go and tell his parents. I'm trying to shove his driver's licence back into his wallet, but there's a bit of screwed-up writing paper stopping it going in properly. I take it out. A phone number. It's almost my mobile number, but with a zero at the end instead of a six. And just like that, I know what's happened. When I scrawled my number on his arm, I didn't write the six properly; probably because I was so wasted. I just stand there in the reception area and let myself cry.

Mrs Locke's eyes are puffy, and she has little spots of mascara in the shadows beneath them, but she smiles when she opens the door, and regards me with expectation.

"Hi, Mrs Locke. Umm, this is a bit random, but I'm James. I'm a friend of Tim's, and I have to tell you something."

Her lip wobbles almost imperceptibly, and she blinks back more tears. "I'm so sorry, umm, James, please excuse me. We're having a rather difficult day already! Please, come in."

I step inside the immaculate new-build and feel my face flush. I hadn't realised how cold I'd been. It's weird, being in the house of the man I love but hardly know, sinking into his parents 'burgundy sofa, when I'm trying to perch on the edge. Mr Locke rolls up his newspaper with quick, long fingers and arranges his features into a smile.

"Steve, this is James. A friend of Tim's."

"Hi," I smile, trying to maintain eye contact, feeling awkward as hell. Why hadn't I just let the hospital ring Tim's parents? "Umm, I'm so sorry. This is a bit difficult! Tim's in hospital. He's going to be okay – don't worry! I found him by the river, unconscious, so I rang an ambulance. They think he's, umm, drunk too much. I think they're pumping his stomach. I brought his wallet – that's how I found out where you live," I say, holding the frayed purple wallet out to Mrs Locke. Her mouth is a line that she's trying to hold straight as she looks at me, conveying her thanks with her gaze, and the tears course silently down her cheeks. She drops her eyes to the floor. Mr Locke stands and comes to take the wallet from me.

"Thank you, James," he says, being the man, touching his wife's shoulder briefly. "I'm afraid we're having rather a bad time with Tim and his sister at present, and I appreciate you coming round. I must ask, though – how do you know Tim? I don't mean to be rude, but I've never seen you before and you're clearly not from round here!"

It's my accent. I stand out like a sore thumb here. I tell him I met Tim at a football match. It's too vague. Mr Locke's stare hardens.

"A football match. I'm going to talk straight with you, James. Are you in any way responsible for Tim being in hospital?"

"No!" I realise I'm on my feet, so I plonk myself back down on the sofa. "No! I just found him! Tim's sound – I'd never do anything to hurt him!"

"Steve, it doesn't matter! After all that happened with his sister, let's just get down to the hospital and be with our son!" Mrs Locke is standing now and walks out into the hall. I follow, apologising, and stand on their bowling green of a lawn while they grab bags and keys and get into their car. Mrs Locke gives me an uncertain smile as her husband reverses the car at speed. Then they are gone. What the fuck do I do now?

Tim

I don't want to go back to my parents 'house when I leave the hospital – not immediately – so James and I end up at the only other place we can go: The Riverboat. At first, I don't recognise the other barman.

"WHAT THE FUCK IS *HE* DOING BEHIND THE BAR?!" I scream at Stuart.

James pulls me back.

"Tim. You have to calm down. You knew he was out of prison. He was going to have to get a job somewhere!" Stuart hisses, staring daggers at me, while Richard gloats as he chops up a lime.

"Don't you dare fucking side with him!" I yell back, wrenching my arm free of James 'grasp. "He killed my sister!"

"What?!" James pulls me round to face him. "What's going on?!"

Stuart is suddenly my side of the bar, guiding me outside. He moves a distraught James away from me with an apologetic smile, telling him, "Leave it, mate – I'll fill you in later." I can see him thinking *who the hell's that?*

Stuart shoves a ready-rolled cigarette into my mouth, then lights his own. "Tim. He didn't. That's just the point. Richard was cleared of all charges …"

I'm more upset than angry now, and I thrust him out of my face, by the shoulders "Well, he might not have slit her wrists, but he made her life hell … he drove her to it!"

"Tim, please. Your sister was ill, you know that. She was severely depressed and she … she took her own life. Everyone knew it, whether they said anything or not. I can only imagine what it must have been like for you, living with her."

I want to smash Stuart's face in, put my fists through the wall, but I know he's right. Sally says I'm projecting all my anger onto Rich, and maybe she's right, but there's something about that bloke that's always got my back up. He's sketchy as fuck, and I hate him. I start to cry, so Stuart kind of pats me on the arm, and walks back into the bar. As he opens the door, I can hear it's all kicking off inside.

A few minutes later, and James is at my side. He flicks his Zippo and places his hand on my shoulder as he holds the flame to my cigarette. The gesture is comforting and warm, and I lean my cheek onto the back of his hand, but only for an instant – if somebody saw us, it'd be all over town in three seconds – and I jerk my head away and take a step back. I see James 'heart break as I do this, and I whisper, "Please, don't! I'll sort it, I promise. Give me time!" I can't face one of these conversations, especially not right now. The white-washed pebbledash pricks my skin. My back is literally against the wall.

Stuart storms out of the bar, finds us, and hisses in my face, "Look, I know you're upset, but say anything like that again, and you're barred. Got it?"

"Look, I'm sorry, mate, but the guy's a wanker. He's dodgy – you know he is."

Stuart calms down a bit, but he's on edge. He's clearly had his work cut out calming people down in there. He pulls a battered pack of Marlboros out of his back pocket, sparks one up, and nods us out to the beer garden.

"Look, mate, I haven't been entirely honest with you. Rich is blackmailing me. He clocked me and Will dealing the other the other day. I can't lose this job, and I can't lose my extra income, either. I'm fucking struggling to put food on the table at the moment. Just leave him be, okay?"

Extra income. "What are you dealing?"

Will knows the drummer from Charcot, who are now widely heralded as the new stars of the UK Indie scene. Apparently, they met on the art foundation course at Exeter College when they were sixteen. I'm so glad I sent that gig review to the *NME* – I'm kind of in with Charcot now, and they're giving me a lot of exclusives. I'm raking it in and it's paying more than the sports reports. James calls it a symbiotic relationship. Charcot signed with an Indie label based in Liverpool, the drummer loved his skunk, and the rest, Will was up there watching a gig one day, got in with a dealer, and now Will's using the link to supply the West Country. They call Exeter *The Gold Mine*. And now here we are, needing money, because James 'student loan is running down and he refuses to ask his parents for help, and they're fucking loaded. To be honest, my folks aren't badly off, but I'm not taking a penny off them, either. I won't give them the satisfaction.

They used to do it all in service station car parks, but that all went boom last year when the police got a tip-off, and some bloke had all his fingers chopped off. It's a fucking hassle, but now the Scousers drive down to Tamehaven, and take it out to this cove, by boat, and then Will canoes round to the cove from the other side and picks it up, and this posh bird who's somehow in with them meets Will in the safe house in Swansburne, where they cut it up and bag it up. It's this dilapidated B & B on Marine Parade, run by an old duck who thinks Will and this Lydia are having an affair. Will can be surprisingly charismatic when he wants to, and he's charmed the old biddy into thinking that they're old flames from school, that Lydia's husband is manipulative and violent, and that the two of them are meeting up when the husband goes away on business and are looking for a place where they can start afresh and working out how she can safely get away from him so they can be together. The hotelier, Grace, has taken pity on Lydia and gives her free coffee – it's hilarious! Will's a fucking good actor, on the sly. Or maybe that's what he really is – sly.

Anyway, the system, though fucking mental (you can tell someone who's fried his brain is calling the shots) is perfect – it'd be criminal not to supply the demand. I was in The Riverboat the other day, and a couple of grockles came in and ended up staying for a liquid lunch. The bloke was picking the label of his bottle of Newkie Brown and chain-smoking, and he said to his girlfriend, "I don't know. This country living is really getting to me. Somebody give me some drugs!"

She replied, "I know! I've never injected before, but I feel I need to!"

If Devon is a gold mine, it's also a fucking quagmire. It's dragged us all down, so we're going to dig our way out. Exploit the natural resources, as it were.

Just as we're getting used to our *second jobs* as we call them, the safe house – the B & B in Swansburne – appears on the news with loads of police cars outside it. The officer in charge makes an embarrassed statement to the press about how they thought it was being used by a major drugs ring, but no evidence of any suspicious activity was found. They believe they have been the victims of an elaborate hoax.

We all breathe a sigh of relief, and laugh at the coppers, but Will is scared, and is taking it seriously. He reckons the police are getting tipped off by someone on the northerners 'side – it sure as hell isn't any of us! Will and Stuart and I have set one up in the cottage James and I are now renting in Belmont Road. It's set off the main drag, and I'd never noticed the cottages up there before and I've lived in this shithole of a town all my life. James comes down every weekend unless I'm up north covering an away match. I tell Sally I'm working, which is partly true, and anyway, as we're not living together, she doesn't know any different. James and I lie low. Literally. I quite like the arrangement – Mum and Dad think they've got a successful son who's with a lovely girlfriend, Sally got me back, so she's happy, and James and I can be together. The only downside is that James wants me to come out – he doesn't want us to have to pretend our relationship's platonic, when it's not. I presume he has come out, but how can I do that to Mum and Dad, after Cath dying? They'd go ballistic. Mum's always on about how much she's going to enjoy being a "glamorous granny". And what the fuck would they say down the pub? They're all homophobic, narrow-minded wankers – they'd rip me to shreds! I'd never be allowed in a press box again! And they certainly wouldn't buy drugs off me … and I need them to buy drugs off me so I can be with James at the weekend. It's fucking catch-22. People might be more tolerant in the big cities – although I doubt it – but down here coming out would be a death sentence. If he loves me, James is just going to have to get on with it. Love's about compromise, isn't it?

James

Friday morning and the sun's out. Everything seems better in the sunshine. I'm on campus, heading for the lab, and the red-brick university buildings shine like they're made of garnet. I stare up the intricate gothic architecture of the clock tower and marvel for the umpteenth time at how the hell they constructed it. I imagine someone my age, right at the top, carving the stone, looking out over the expanding city, trying to pick out his house, trying to concentrate on the wages he'll receive rather than how many seconds he would fall before his body splashes and shatters on the stone floor, trusting in Bertie to keep him safe. Unless the Liver Building hadn't been built then. I wonder if you can smell the sea from up there. The clock chimes nine, startling me, and the group of girls sitting in the sunshine, where my imaginary lad would have fallen, laugh at me. I blush and try to focus on the module we're starting this morning. Cancer. This is one of the reasons I chose this course: when my best mate, Andy, was thirteen, his dad died of lung cancer. He'd never smoked a cigarette in his life. Everyone was saying things like *when your time's up, your time's up* and *it's probably because of all the pollution.* People were hugging Andy, saying how sorry they were, how his dad was such a great bloke, how he didn't need this sort of shit happening to him after what had happened to his leg, and when he'd not long moved up north. And then after the funeral, that was it. His dad was old news. I was the only one who decided to do anything about it. And when I went to uni, Andy moved back down to Devon. He said there was no point being in a place he hardly knew, without his best mate. He was quite depressed, and really angry with the world. When I go down to Eskwich to be with Tim, I often think I should go round to Andy's – just turn up on his doorstep – but I know he wouldn't like that. He never replies to my letters any more. Maybe he's moved. And now I'm thinking of Tim again. Fuck's sake.

I've been mulling things over for days. It's all I think about – does he want me, or doesn't he want me? I'd like to have that punch-in-the-gut realisation that I've never been more than an experiment – a fuck-up – to him, when he was bladdered; that he doesn't love me, never loved me, never will love me. But I know that's not true. I actually know that he loves me, and I should be made up; but I'm not. It is simply painful. It hurts me, of course, but it also hurts me on his behalf. He's never true to himself. He prefers to hide behind this facade of a relationship with Sally, and that he's the hard man, the lad, getting bladdered and rowdy, out with the boys, and I know that that's what this alcohol thing is – it's a way of blacking it all out so he doesn't have to think about it. A coping mechanism. Even though it's not really coping. This way, he doesn't have to face his parents and tell them, or his scummy mates. This way, he doesn't have to break up with Sally. It's denial. It's fear. It's pathetic.

I couldn't concentrate in labs, even after a couple of Red Bulls, and I'm so pissed off with myself. And now I have to raid my student loan again and get the train down to Devon to have a dirty weekend with Tim. And that's all it is. I should just break it off with him, concentrate on my degree. What the hell am I doing?

The train slows as we approach Eskwich Parkway. The station is nowhere near Eskwich, so I'm going to have to get the bus into town. I don't think Tim appreciates how much of an effort all this travelling is. He says I can work on the train, but I find that really hard. I love watching how the landscape changes from the harshness of the North and the Black Country to the lazy greenness of Devon. It's like ripples in a pond, but only physically – emotionally, it's the other way round, and I go over what I'm going to say to Tim when I get back to the cottage. Deep breaths. This is it.

"James!" I don't have to turn around to know it's Tim on the platform, but I do, and when I see his smile, I'm made up and my resolve just ebbs away. Like ripples in a pond.

Will

It's on the front page of *The Sun. CHARCOT DOPE IN DOPE WAR!*

The hospital are treating Rob – their lead singer - for sepsis; the police want to arrest him for possession with intent to supply. What a fucking idiot. We'd been having a couple of beers in Abercromby Square, while I waited for one of my skunk-head students. Charcot were doing a gig at the Philharmonic as a favour to the SU events team who had supported them so much in their really early days, so Rob was hanging out with me on the grass, talking at a hundred miles an hour about how Rose was such an apt name for his girlfriend, with all its connotations, and he just started skinning up on autopilot. I clocked the lad in the grey hoody giving us a shifty look as he walked down the path to the dome building thingy, but when he got there, he pulled a book out of his rucksack, along with a folder and a pen, so I assumed he was just a chilling out after lectures. My student turned up, sat down with us, chatted while he smoked a Marlboro, we did the deal and off he went. I was all up for going back to the B & B, but Rob was pretty stoned now, waxing lyrical about Bach's Toccata in D major or something, and how he loved the clock tower because it was so spiky, like a load of glass shards sparkling red like they'd absorbed the lifeblood of the people who erected it; he didn't want to go, so I thought, *fuck it,* and skinned up myself, and lay on the parched grass, cloud-watching, thinking about which train to catch so I could be back for work on Monday morning. The clock struck half eight, so I got up, kicked Rob, who'd closed his eyes and was mouthing words, and told him they'd be shutting the gates soon.

"Yeah, we've got half an hour. Take a chill pill, man," he slurred, without opening his eyes, so I sort of floated through treacle back to my B & B – this shit was *strong* – and left him there.

Half an hour later, I hear arguing downstairs. The room I've been allocated is directly above what passes for reception, and instinct makes me take out my earphones so I can hear better. It's Rob. He's desperate to get in, but the landlady won't let him. She's talking and shouting about phoning the *bizzies*, and he's yelling *but I've been stabbed!* I rush out of my room and down the mottled blue carpet and arrive in reception to hear her shouting about how *you druggies have got it coming to you – you reap what you sow,* and demanding he get out of her house – and some bloke who's built like a brick shithouse barges me out of the way and shoves Rob violently backwards – Rob stumbles over the rug, screaming *he's going to kill me!* but the bloke and his wife are just yelling *get out of my house!* And suddenly there are sirens, and Rob scrambles up from the floor and starts running up the road, but a copper thunders up behind him and catches him before he makes the corner. We're all out on the street – everyone is out on the street – and I'm running up to Rob, but the copper has got him, the cuffs are on, and Rob is half marched, half dragged back to the police car. As he passes me, he is pale as fuck, and the sight of the blood oozing down his arm from a rip in his black T-shirt, makes me urge. Rob's eyes are wild – too wide, but still bloodshot, and he tries to keep eye contact with me as the copper pulls him by. Rob says, "What the fuck is this shit? The cunt stabbed me with his front door key!"

Then he turns to the copper, shouting, "A fucking student in a grey hoodie stabbed me with a fucking door key! Go and look for him! It's him you should be arresting, not me!"

The copper pushes down on the top of Rob's head so he

doesn't bang it on the roof of the car, squashing the red spikes of his hair, and then they are gone. I watch the police car ease its way round the corner, and when I turn around there's another copper standing behind me. She asks me if I know Rob, and instinct makes me answer, "No, but I think he's that bloke from that band." The landlady apologises for the commotion and warns me that there are loads of druggies round here, rival gangs and all sorts, and it's affecting her business. She tells me that just the other night, they heard a load of helicopters above their house, and then a policeman came and knocked on their door and told everyone on the street to stay inside and lock their door and windows until the police gave the all-clear, because there'd been a lethal stabbing because someone had been dealing on someone else's patch, and the culprit was running around Toxteth, armed and dangerous.

As I turn to go back to my room, the realisation that this could be the downfall of a lucrative operation and loads of fucking hard work, hits me, and I just stand there with my mouth open, so fucking glad that I'd had a shower and used my eye drops.

Adam

Less than an hour into my shift, one of the security guys placed his meaty hand on my shoulder and frogmarched me to the office. Things were pretty hazy, but I felt good, even though I could tell there was something wrong. I kept it light, chatting to the bloke about the girl who works in the canteen, about how we worked so hard we ought to be paid more, about us on the frontline versus the bosses sitting behind their comfy desks, raking it in, speculating about whether Mr Farefield was going to sit me down in a comfy leather chair and offer me whiskey in a crystal glass … But the security guy just gave me a tight smile and said nothing.

"Oh, hi!" Kayleigh jumps up off the sofa and hugs me.

"You're home early!" I can't return the hug. I stand there like a statue in her arms until she says, "You stink of booze. Have you been to the pub?" She steps back, her hands on my waist, and I just stand there looking at this beautiful girl with her wild hair, who I loved so much, and I feel the panic rise. As if on cue, Liam stirs from where he's fallen asleep on the sofa. How can I tell her I've lost my job for being 'under the influence in the workplace'? How the fuck are we going to support a kid on her part-time job in the hippy shop? I blink back tears and remember that this is all his fault. No. Actually, it's all Kayleigh's fault. I shouldn't have come home.

"Yeah," I say, going with the lie as it comes out of me. "They got muddled up at work and thought me and Chris had swapped shifts. They told me to go home coz we're not legally allowed to work sixteen hours in twenty-four, so I thought I'd go to the pub until you came home, then I got distracted – you know what it's like!" I give her that smile and add, "Do you fancy an early night?"

"Bloody hell, Adam, it's only just gone seven, and I was going through my Book of Shadows ..." Kayleigh trails off, and I glance behind and notice that the coffee table is chock-a-block with candles and notebooks. A load of joss stick ash falls onto a patch of bare wood with a soft clap.

Anger of thwarted desire flares up in me for a second, but I realise this means I can go back out and talk to Stuart. I have a business proposition for him.

Will

"You dropped five hundred quid's worth of skunk down a fucking drain?!"

"What could I do, man? They were chasing me! I would have gone down if they'd caught me with all that! Anyway, it was in a bag! When you go back to the B & B, just fish it out! I dropped it between the black Beemer and the yellow Metro. It was a fucking good shot, actually!" Rob giggles, but I'm not laughing.

"You fucking twat! You know I can't be seen with you again, don't you? How the fuck is this operation gonna work now?" I kick the back of the phone box, and some rust drops off the shelf. "You owe me five hundred quid. I don't care how you get it to me, but I want my money."

"Come on, man!" Rob coaxes, the giggle in his tone fading a little. "It's done wonders for our image – it's sex and drugs and rock 'n 'roll, isn't it! Charcot have hit the big time! I've done you a fucking favour! Anyway, we've been mates for years! And you've got hundreds more contacts through me, and been to a million gigs …"

"Oh, yeah – you're such a fucking big shot! How altruistic of you, helping out a poor no-hoper mate from school …" I lose my thread, I'm so fucking angry, and something like shame creeps in. "I don't need your fucking pity, *mate*!" Slamming the handset back into its holder, I storm out of the phone box and head back to the B & B on Croxteth Road. I need to get out of Liverpool, sharpish.

In spite of myself, my brisk walk calms me, and when I splash through the dirty puddles by the street sign, I actually saunter on past the B & B, and up the road a bit. There's no black Beemer parked up, but there is a battered yellow Metro City, and I think I remember seeing it in that place before. The back driver's side wheel half covers a drain. The laces of my Converse trainers are loose – I have to have them like that because the tongue sometimes rubs on the top of my foot and gives me blisters – and one of them is dragging on the pavement, grey and wet, so I stop to tie it. What else can I do? I can see something off-white floating amongst fag butts and leaves. It can only be the bag of dope. But how the fuck am I going to get it out without being noticed?

I tie the lace, walk on, and pop into the corner shop at the very end of the road to buy a pack of Marlboros. By the till, they've got the usual rack of sweets to piss off the parents who've only gone in to get a paper. There are some of those insanely bouncy balls, some keyrings, and also a box of animal heads on sticks. If you pull the end of the stick, the gaping mouth of the shark (for example) closes. I buy one *for my mate's little boy.* It doesn't have to be a lie. I'm sure Liam would love a present from his Uncle Will.

And by some fucking miracle, I get the dope! I fish it out of a drain with a fucking toy shark! I get it, but I'm not going to tell Rob – he can pay me the five hundred quid; it's not going to hurt him. I pick up my stuff and check out of the B & B – the landlady says it's been nice to have a quiet lad like me stay with them, instead of the usual gobshites – and head for Lime Street. I have to change trains at Birmingham New Street, and as usual, there's a delay, thanks to Maggie privatising the railways, so I grab a Burger King, and ring Rob's mobile. He's repentant. He's got an idea for how he can get the money to me, and how we can continue the operation. Apparently, he got the idea from a student at the gig in Liverpool (they were allowed to play a week later – it was too lucrative for the SU not to. Funny how money forgives crimes), who was reading *Jamaica Inn* at the bar.

James

On Saturday, it's just the two of us staying in, watching the Jean-Luc Picard trilogy: *Generations, First Contact,* and then *Insurrection.* We're drinking Cava instead of beer, because it kind of feels like we've come back together from being a great distance apart, and we start the moment we wake. I'm snug – there's no better word for it – under our duvet that's too many togs for the weather, and sleepy after sex, so I let Tim go down and make breakfast. He comes back up with the Cava and a bacon sandwich on a tray, and that sets the tone for the day. And it's boss; we hardly move from the bedroom all day. At about seven, Tim orders a Chinese for dinner, and we talk about our plans, over fortune cookies and spring rolls. I like the cottage, with its small, uneven-walled rooms, and the wood burner in the front room; the garden's a mess, but that's no big deal – we have time. If I got a job at the University of Exeter, we could live here and commute. I put all this to Tim, who smiles, but says he was looking forward to getting out of Dodge and into the big city. He talks about going for a job on the *Liverpool Echo.* In the end, we compromise and decide to look for jobs in London. After all, that's where all the money is.

On Sunday, we're woken at eight-thirty by angry banging at the door. Tim drags himself out from the covers, kneels against the headboard and looks out of the open window.

"Will! What the fuck?!" he hisses, and with a glance and a roll of his eyes at me, he goes downstairs. I lie there for a bit, then curiosity gets the better of me, and I pull on my jeans and a T-shirt and pad downstairs. Our kitchen floor is tiled, and the sudden drop in temperature makes me shiver. Tim and Will stare at me, and it takes a beat before I realise what I've done. I recover the situation by saying, "What the fuck, man?" to Will, and "Morning, mate, thanks for letting me crash last night," to Tim. Then I pick up the kettle, wave it in their general direction and say, "I'll put the kettle on, shall I?" Situation diffused.

Then Will starts talking about the ramifications of Rob from Charcot getting busted in Liverpool. I've been so wrapped up in myself, my head's been so full of Tim, that I haven't watched the news or got a paper in weeks. I turn to Tim. "Why didn't you say anything?" and now it's his turn to look sheepish, and I realise what this weekend has been all about, why he picked me up from the station, brought me Cava in bed for breakfast – he'd known this had been coming. Will explains to us how he's going to be collecting the drops from now on – one of our Liverpool connections will drive down to Devon, stay in a different

B & B each time, and drop the drugs in a bit of cliff face at Smuggler's Cove, near Tamehaven. Then Tim or me, or Adam, will be visiting Tamehaven Wildlife Conservation Centre, and walk down the tunnel to Smuggler's Cove after, and pick it up. It'll involve buying a bag or a pyjama case or similar from the zoo each time, but it's a safe way of continuing. He's telling us what's going to happen, and my hackles should be up, but it's so fucking unlikely, it's brilliant, and I laugh. "Sounds like something out of *Jamaica Inn!*" I comment. Will freezes and says, "Yeah. That's where Rob got the idea."

And Tim's tone is icy as he says, "Adam as in Adam Brooks? What the fucking hell has he got to do with it?"

"Just between you, me and the lamp post, he's lost his job, he can't pay the rent, and he won't tell Kayleigh about it. Stuart's given him a part-time job in The Riverboat, doing early mornings and Wednesdays in the kitchen, so Kayleigh and her mates won't see him. It's shady as fuck but needs must."

Will pauses, and glances into the front room. "Oh. You didn't kip on the sofa, then?" he says to me. "Tim, you didn't put the poor bloke in that box you call a spare room, did you? His feet must have been dangling out the door all night!"

"I was in the attic room, actually," I retort. "It's huge. And lovely and warm."

Will picks up on it immediately. His eyes flash. "Attic room, eh? How warm is 'warm'?"

Justin, the drummer from Charcot has a side-line shop in Tamehaven – a tattoo and piercing studio that also sells bongs and legal highs. That's where we get the hydroponic equipment. By virtue of the fact that I'm a biochemist and a lab technician, I get the job of setting it all up.

It's fun. And gardening is something I've enjoyed since childhood. This is a blessing, because for the first time ever, I feel that Will has accepted me – when there's no one else in the room, we can actually have a conversation. The other day, Will turned up when Tim was reporting on an Eskwich Town football match. I could tell he was surprised that I opened the door to what was – ostensibly – Tim's cottage, but then he is perceptive. He's got a depth to him that most people don't see behind the facade of bitterness and alcoholism. I was making a side salad to go with our steak that evening, and I was topping it with scoops of avocado.

"You're actually posh as fuck, James," he observed.

"No I'm not! I just like growing them."

"You grow avocados?"

"Well, I've never actually got to the point where they fruit, but I've grown plenty of trees. My parents have a house down between Swansburne and Tamehaven, right on top of a cliff, and the conservatory has 360-degree light, so I took one of my trees down there. Also, it was partly because it was in a massive pot and our cat kept shitting in it! Anyway, it grew to about eight foot. Then my folks didn't go down there for a while, so it didn't get watered, and that was the end of that!"

Will laughs. "Yeah, I tried to grow alpines at the far end of my garden, so I needed pretty gritty soil. I went outside the morning after I'd planted it up, and it looked like every cat in Farefield had been for a shit in it. Fucking cats!" He pauses. "You're going into your final year in October, aren't you?"

"Yes," I reply, taking the can of Krony he's now holding out to me.

"So why aren't you in Liverpool, studying? Why are you down here, growing weed?" Excepting the part about the weed, that's exactly what my parents have been saying – *just stay in Liverpool and get your degree, James!*

"It's fun. I enjoy it – it's kind of relaxing. And I need the extra cash."

Will swigs the dregs of his beer and takes another out of the fridge. I'm torn – I'm glad we're finally getting on, but I know Tim will be pissed off when he comes home and sees half his Krony is gone. "Can't your folks help you out?"

My smile is more of a grimace. "Umm, they got a cob on and we kind of fell out. They wouldn't let me go to the university I wanted to. But I'm lucky – I have a student grant. The government are looking to abolish them – I don't know how students in the future will ever get themselves out of debt."

Will lets out a bitter laugh. "Most of them'll smoke weed to forget about it and get through the days, like the rest of the world!" He pauses. "Unless they have a bit of imagination and an attic, then they'll deal, like us. You sink or swim in life, James. I chose to swim."

He turns his back on me, goes to the fridge and snaps out another can of Tim's Krony. "Want another one?"

"Umm, no thanks, we're about to have dinner."

Will laughs again. "Are you two fucking married or something?" he jokes. He takes a long drink of Krony, places the can on the table and looks me straight in the eye. "Or are you just fucking?"

Tim

The kitchen is electric with the tension between James and Will. There's a long moment where my mind skips ahead with all the things they could have been talking about, but Will interrupts my thoughts with, "Tim, did you know that James 'family own the holiday home on top of Shell Cove?"

There's a pause. It's fucking tense. Will's smile stretches into a line so thin, it's cruel. He's looking straight at James. "And did you know that you can only get to Horse Cove on foot once a year when the tide is right? Otherwise it's a boat trip. It's pretty much inaccessible. I know trainspotters like to take photos of it, because the railway line goes in and out of tunnels all the way down the coast, but they have to stand on the cliffs – they can't actually get there. Isn't that interesting, Tim?" His tone is so cold, I shiver.

"Umm, yeah, but your folks have pretty much abandoned you, haven't they?" I say to James, searching his pale, frightened face. "Anyway, it's Horse Cove, isn't it?" The atmosphere is so charged, I can't not ask, "Has something happened? What's going on?"

"You're a smart lad, Tim, standing there in your suit with your briefcase and your career. You're just like your boyfriend." He cocks his head towards James. "I'm sure you two can figure it out. 'Make it so', as it were." He smirks and takes a can – the last can! – of my beer out of the fridge and stalks out of the house. "Here's to swimming, not sinking," he says as he brushes past me. "Cheers!"

Richard

It's actually brilliant having a maisonette up the road from the pub. Especially when most people think you're in prison and never coming out. Yes, the story was all over the news, but this town is full of wankers who get their knowledge of current affairs through Deadenders and bloody *Coronation Street*. It's nice to sit up here in the dark, in silence, my back against the sash window which is open a crack, and listen to them all stumbling home, talking too loudly, shouting, arguing, fighting. It appears that the brother of my darling dead girlfriend is growing weed in a cottage in Belmont Road. The golden boy, big-shot journalist, Tim Locke, is a liar, just like everybody else. Oh, how the mighty have fallen – or are about to fall!

Will

Adam is a fucking liability. He's also an idiot. What the fuck has Kayleigh seen in him all these years?! He doesn't get the fact that you can't sell drugs if you're caning them all the time! They're not free to us: we're the handlers – this is business, a means to an end. It's fucking punk rock. Every man for themselves. Survival of the fittest.

I park my Polo in Marine Parade and just sit there, watching the drizzle softly cover my windscreen as *Kare Kare* fades out. The CD must have been round a few times during the drive down, but I haven't heard any of it. For the millionth time today, I wonder why I am surrounded by idiots, then think that really, I've surrounded myself with them, because I need them. I wish I could just fuck society and do it all on my own. At least then I'd have control. It's so stressful trying to manage them all. Stuart's doing a roaring side trade in The Riverboat, which is great for all of us, but he's being overly flash with his cash. He's buying girls drinks all over the place, and his usual Matalan jeans have been conspicuously replaced by Levi 501s. I keep telling him to rein it in, but he just gives me this sarcastic grin and says *what's the use in having money if you can't spend it?*

She doesn't know it – or at least she doesn't show that she does – but I'm using my money to pay the shortfall in Kayleigh's rent. I hoped that by telling Adam about her going off to see Richard, it would split them up, and she'd realise who she should be with: someone who can take care of her, who looks out for her, who has her best interests at heart – me. I'd raise her kid. I know she says Liam is Adam's, but neither of us can get away from the fact that he could easily be mine. Whenever I see Liam, I'm looking for pieces of myself in him. And he likes me! I bought him some Crayola crayons the other day, and he virtually tore them out of their box, grabbed the nearest bit of paper – last week's free paper – clenched the red one in his sticky little fist and started scribbling. He looked so happy, half sitting, half lying on the dirty carpet of their front room, that I actually felt happy for the first time since Kayleigh and I rowed out to Horse Cove. The acknowledgement of that fact was like a punch in the gut. I'd glanced up at Kayleigh, who was bringing our coffee in from the kitchen, and her eyes were filled with so much love for him, I almost got down on one knee and proposed. I heard my voice say, "I love … this song." And she'd laughed so much, she spilt coffee on the floor. It was *Wonderwall.* She knows I hate Oasis.

An HST rushes by, too fast to be stopping at Swansburne station. It must be the fifth train to pass in as many minutes. People are getting on with their lives. I need to be getting on with mine. I get out of the car and pick up the Toffee Crisp wrapper that's got tangled up in my flares. Kayleigh always says my car is a tip. I shove too much change into a parking meter that gives nothing back, throw the ticket onto the dashboard, lock the car and trudge up to the bridge. I need to be seen in Swansburne not doing anything dodgy; parking here and walking like I love the sea, that this is my favourite place to be, and The Marine Tavern is my local-away-from-home, and I am fond of it and it is not a complete dated, gloomy shithole where they don't clean the lines often enough. I do the same thing each time – park here, walk out to Cardinal's Cove, stand resting my legs against the low, yellowing sea wall and watch the seabirds on the rock and the surf splashing over semi-exposed rock pools. At the moment, there are two cormorants on the rock. One has its wings splayed open and is facing out to sea, the other has just caught some creature, and is pecking it apart right in front of my face. Grossed out, I make my way past the beach huts, past the dingy cafe and its 'Jolly ' Roger flag, down the slope and onto the sand. Or 'gravel', as almost everyone I know calls it. Adam, the twat, says he hates Swansburne, because the sand is coarse and red, but what else would it be? The ocean batters the cliffs here, breaking off chunks and smashing them into sand. There's a park at the top of the cliffs, and from the beach you can see the deep, thick roots of centuries-old trees, that have been exposed by the erosion. It puts things in perspective. Even at low tide, the sea isn't far from the craggy land. The stone slope onto the beach is topped with slate which makes it slippery in the mizzle, so I tread carefully. The frayed bottoms of my jeans are already soaked dark. Seaweed tidemarks trace patterns across the sand, and, hugging the cliffs, I follow them the length of the cove. Trains whizz in and out of the tunnels either side. Sally used to wave at them when we were kids; she and Dom loved the short journey to Tamehaven, especially in stormy weather when the waves would crash over the sea wall and spray – and occasionally bash – the coaches. Who was it who said that saltwater cures everything?

I stop abruptly. There's a skinny, dark-haired lad crunched up on the sand, picking up stones and half-heartedly throwing them towards the water. It's Dom. Fuck! He's sitting where the damp, rained-on sand meets the wet, with his back to me. I could head back now, and never have to speak to him. Swansburne was always going to be a risk because he's living in a halfway house here, recovering from his latest breakdown. Sally says he's doing well, and I know she and Mum and Dad have been down here and taken him out for fish and chips, but this is the first time I've seen him here. I need to move, but I'm torn between going for the walk I need to be seen going on, and avoiding my brother. I step backwards until my back is against the cliff face, as if my red hair would act as camouflage. Movement draws my gaze left, to the slate slope; a girl comes onto the beach. I make my decision and continue with my walk – I'll smile at her on the way back.

There's a long stone groin or seawall or whatever jutting out into the bay – presumably to protect the railway – and it creates currents which almost split the cove in two. At the far side of the cove, sheltered by the wall, the sand is pushed higher, and you find shells here, and smooth, sort of calico stones, some of which remind me of bones. The cliff face here is masked with wet, mossy stuff, and run-off drips into a pool at its foot. I know that just behind here, on the right day, James will have stashed the canoe. On impulse, I turn away, crunch down to the water's edge, and gaze across the bay.

"Will!"

Shit. That was a mistake. Dom is standing up waving at me, and the goth girl is standing close to him, smoking. I give them a limp wave in return and am now obliged to go over and talk to them.

"All right, bruvver?" Dom says, holding a rollie out to me. At least he had the sense not to try to shake my hand or hug me.

"Fine, thanks. You?"

"Yeah." There's a pregnant pause. I look at the girlfriend, who immediately stares at the sand. "I just don't get why you're walking about in Swansburne all the time, but you never come and see me. Anyone would think you're ashamed of me."

I shrug. I can't lie.

Fire blazes in Dom's eyes. "You're a fucking bastard, Will," he states. "If I had an amputated leg, or diabetes, or – I don't know – Down's syndrome or something, you'd be okay with that. Because those are 'proper 'illnesses, aren't they? Why can't you accept that someone might have a chemical imbalance in their brain, and ..."

"The only reason you have a 'chemical imbalance 'in your brain, is because you smoke too much fucking weed and can't handle the fact that you're responsible for your life! You can talk about Art-with-a-capital-A and Nietzsche and all that crap, but Mum and Dad aren't going to baby you forever – at some point you're just going to have to get on with it like the rest of us!"

Dom stares daggers at me, and I notice the girl is reaching for his hand. Skin brushes skin, and he turns to her and mouths something. The girl glances at me before making her way quickly back towards the slope.

"You're fucking chaos, Dom! You just cause trouble everywhere you go, because you live in a fucking fantasy world! Grow the fuck up!"

"Fuck, fuck, fuckety fuck," Dom laughs. "I've seen you, you know. With your little canoe. I heard you shagging that girl on the beach; it sounded like she was faking, to me."

I could kill him. I could knock him out, drag him into the sea, and hold his scrawny face under the water …

"What are you going to do for me, then, bruvver?" Dom says. "What's it going to take to keep me quiet?"

"What do you want?" I hiss through clenched teeth.

He smiles. "Well, I'd like a bottle of vodka for tonight, and then I want in."

"I'll get you some vodka, but you're not getting involved in this."

"Okay, well, I'm sure the police would be interested in your new-found hobby."

We stare at each other. I remember the little boy on the train, squealing with delight as we pop in and out of tunnels, playing 'off-ground tap 'with him in the front room. Nicking half-penny sweets from the corner shop … Dom's expression softens. "Please, Will," he asks, "these meds are dumbing me down, but I have to take them to get out of the system. I can't paint, I can't do fucking anything but sit staring into space. I want to be sharp again. Please, Will. If you can get any coke or speed – any uppers – I need them. I really do." Saltwater blurs my vision.

"All right. Just don't say fucking anything to anyone." I slip my hand into the pocket of my denim jacket. There's a hole in it, and in the lining is my emergency wrap of coke. I mock-shake Dom's hand and slip him the wrap. "And try not to cane it." I make to walk off, but Dom follows.

"There's an offie round the corner from the toilets," he says.

Richard

"Kayleigh!"

She jumps and drops her carrier bag. She doesn't need to look round, but I don't move; I stand there and watch her pick up her Granny Smith apples and a jar of coffee that's about to roll into the road. Then she turns to me, pale as fuck. Her mass of hair blows in her face, but it doesn't hide the tears that are already coursing down her cheeks.

"What do you want, Richard?"

"Just my stuff, thanks, Kayleigh. I'll walk with you. Unless you fancy a swift half in The Riverboat." She shakes her head and we walk the short way down Thomas Street. She shivers, and I wonder if she's having one of her flashbacks.

"Mum's coming back with Liam in an hour," she states, dropping her bag and keys and walking into the kitchen. I follow her.

"That's okay, I'm not staying long. I'll just grab as much as I can and drop it back to mine and come back for the rest another day.

"Actually, I think you owe me something else, don't you, Kayleigh? I mean, I was in a cell, on my own, for a long time, and you were the one who put me there. It was all your fault, Kayleigh – you do know that, don't you? I actually did nothing wrong, but everyone hates me anyway … and I'm having to prove myself all over again. Mud sticks, you know. And I'm not getting any comfort from anyone."

As I've moved forward, she's backed off. I give her shoulders a little push, and she falls back onto the bed.

Will

It's the sort of day when you hear people commenting to each other as they saunter around, *when the sun's out, Devon's as good as anywhere.* Twats! Yes, the view is pretty – I'm not going to deny that – but, honestly? –

Cardinal's Cove as good as Mauritius? Come on!

I'm lying on the smooth stone wall adjacent to the ramshackle cafe, chain-smoking a pack of Marlboros. I can see pretty much all of the cove from here, as well as the length of the walkway-cum-promenade bit that stretches between Cardinal's and Boat Cove, as well as the smattering of old folks sitting on the cafe chairs, shivering over their Styrofoam cups of tea. It's late afternoon, and the families are coming off the beach so that they're home in time for the kids 'bath and bed. If Kayleigh and I were here, we'd be leaving now. We'd probably grab an ice cream on the way back to the car, and then I'd carry an exhausted, sand-encrusted Liam the rest of the way. A cool breeze is picking up, and I can picture it whipping Kayleigh's tangly hair into her face, and probably her ice cream as well, and she'd be laughing, and I'd be laughing, and Liam would be heavy and warm and floppy in his slumber, and – get a fucking grip, Whiley! She's not here, Liam's not your kid, and the only way you're going to get out of this shithole of a country is by making some serious money, so fucking concentrate!

I scan the walkway – a few sad middle-aged couples, trying to rekindle their long-dead romance. I scan the chairs – just one old duck in a green duffel coat, staring out to sea with her dead, glassy eyes; and an ageing rocker, smoking a pipe, like a mummified Rick Parfitt. I scan what I can see of the cove – three families, packing up. It's hard to tell whose kids are whose. And a saddo waving a metal detector about. He'd be better off doing that in Exmouth – you hardly even get shells washed up here, let alone anything interesting. Crucially, there's no sign of Dom, or his goth girlfriend.

I finish my sixth fag, neck a can of tepid Coke, and start off down the slope. The girl in the café asks me if I want anything else, because she's just about to shut up shop, and I shake my head. She smiles at me, and I wonder what she meant.

The tide is as far out as I've ever seen it, and although the breeze is cold, it's bloody hot when you're in the sun. The coarse, reddish-brown sand is covered with swirls of crispy seaweed, leaves, and sticks and beach nuts from the trees on top of the cliffs. I remember it being really painful on my feet when I'd run around here as a kid, chasing Sally with dead bits of crabs that didn't make it out of the rockpools. The beach slopes steeply down to the sea, and the usually hidden rocks are exposed, all red and green and glistening. Adult gulls glide low, their squeaking offspring in hot pursuit. I mooch along the line where the dryish sand becomes wet, and cross the cove. The seaweed here is wet, and it stinks. I stand and watch the waves break, row after white-crested row, before I realise my feet are sinking in the sand, and my Connies are getting soaked. When will these bloody people go home?!

The distance between here and Horse Cove is so small, I consider swimming it. It's a tiny stretch of water. But then, once you're in the sea, the waves suddenly look taller, the ocean itself looks bigger, and you can feel the pull of the currents. Also, I don't know where the rocks are, and I don't want to be smashed against the cliffs. I imagine myself, torn and bleeding. And what would I say if someone had to rescue me? No way. Too dangerous. Also, I'm shit-scared of basking sharks – just thinking about their gaping, toothless mouths coming towards me makes me shudder. I'm right at the end of the seawall now. The sun has disappeared behind the cliffs, and the cove is, finally, deserted. I scramble up the wall and reach for the rope and the canoe. James made us get a burgundy one, so that it's kind of camouflaged against the rock – just in case anyone sees it and wonders what it's there for. Not that anyone would. It's only the rich fuckers who have speedboats or jet-skis who can get close enough to see it anyway – so basically James 'family. Swansburne is a fucking dive – it's

Tamehaven where they do the regatta, and Exmouth where there's proper sand. You don't come here unless you were born here, or something's gone seriously wrong in your life.

As my feet are already wet, I don't bother taking off my shoes – I just wedge myself into the canoe, and push off into the water, trying not to think of the night I came here with Kayleigh. The sea looked blue from the shore, but once you're in the water, you can see it's really ruddy-brown and full of sticks, like the beach. I splash out in as straight a line as I can manage with the current and the waves breaking seemingly randomly about the cliffs. I shudder again, this time at the dark shapes of what I hope are rocks beneath me. I've really got to force my way round into cove – I can't believe Kayleigh didn't notice me breaking into a sweat that night. After what seems like ages, there's the swishing of the bottom of the boat on the sand. I haul myself out and drag the canoe up the beach and away from the water. The light is fading quickly now, so I don't hang about. I head for the sound of falling water, pulling my gloves on as I go, pick my way over to it and behind it, climb up and reach for the parcel I know will be in the crevice. It's heavy, and packed tight with what the Scousers call 'ched'. I stand just out of the reach of the splash of the dropping water and look around. I'd love to just make a little shed here, and live in it, like a willing and eager Robinson Crusoe. I'd catch fish, and fry up the seaweed, and sometimes paddle round to Swansburne for bottles of water – then I remember that James 'family have access to this beach. Fuckers! They don't even come from Devon, and they've built a bloody great mansion right on the edge of the cliff, which spoils the coastline for everyone else. I hope the hole in the ozone layer does get bigger – and quickly – and the whole place crashes into the sea when the cliff erodes or there's a tsunami or something. And I'm suddenly aware of the slap of oars on water.

I make to hide behind the waterfall, but remember the canoe is on the beach. Why the fuck didn't I row out in my gloves?! I run behind the pointing rock and get as far as I can behind it, but there's no need, because I can hear Dom shouting, "Will!"

"Will! Where the fuck are you? I know you're here – I saw you rowing out! Will!" He walks over to my canoe. "If you don't come out right now, I'll put a fucking hole in your boat!"

"What's your problem, man?!" I hiss, stepping out of the shadows. I storm over to him and grab him by the shoulders. "You shouldn't fucking be here! And where did you get that fucking canoe?!

"I nicked one from the racks at Boat Cove. And I wouldn't be here, but I need some more coke, and you never answer your phone! I'm feeling great – I've been drawing again for the first time in ages – I could *help* you, with this, Will! I want in!"

"I already told you – No!" I shout in his face and start to drag my canoe down to the water.

"Fine! Whatever! But you *have* to give me some, Will! Is that it?" He points at the package I'm trying to stuff into the waiting Tesco bag in the back of the boat.

I try to get a grip – there's no point arguing with him and shouting at him – he's not going to back down. All I can do is try to fob him off with promises and alcohol again, but he's not having any of it, and then everything happens in slow motion, but it feels like I'm wading through treacle, and I can't react quickly enough.

Dom's pulling the Tesco bag out of my canoe – I'm wedging my legs in and pushing off from the sand – there's a slap, and a scream from him as I smash his hand with the oar again and again – he lets go of the handle and I shove away into deeper water, but he's in the sea up to his waist now, hands slipping as he tries to get a grip on the back of the boat – I whack him again, but the breeze picks up again and the handle of the bag flies up and he grabs it and catches it with the tips of his wet finger, but he's pulled too hard – the top of the bag gapes into the water and we hear a plop and a splash, and Dom is shouting, grappling about in the water, and I'm trying to extricate myself from the canoe and turn round, but we both know it's too late – the coke was wrapped up tight, but not water-tight – and I imagine the powder soaking up the water and getting heavier and heavier, and I'm out of the canoe and we're both in the water, gasping and grunting and the waves are crashing all around and the light has almost gone and I am soaked to the skin – Dom's head disappears beneath the water, and I'm close enough to push it under further, and angry enough to force it down and keep it down, and his hair sweeps along my palm and I can feel the heat of his head through the cold water – and I am so angry, but his arm flies up – he's clutching a dark square thing, and I know it's my coke so hope tears my hand away from his head and pulls the package from his dripping hand. We struggle back to the shore, gasping for breath. Water pours from my hair and my nose as I crawl onto the sand, and I turn back out to see that my canoe is way out of reach. Dom flops onto his back on the sand, laughing, and I punch him in the face. His canoe is only a one-man. I imagine a basking shark, choking on the Tesco bag stuck in its gills.

We're picking our way up the roughly cut steps in the cliff face in near darkness, Dom's canoe stashed behind the pointing rock until we can get rid of it tomorrow. My hands are cut from grabbing the brambles to steady myself, but I don't curse or cry out. Nor does Dom. The only sounds are the waves, the wind and our breath. When we make the top, Dom slaps me as hard as he can on the back. "Got to admit, bruv – that was quite a rush!" I think about shoving him back down the cliff or punching him until every bone in his body snaps, but I haven't got the energy. The only thing we can do is get to James 'house, hope he's there, hope he lets us in, and try to sort this mess out. Through waves of panic, I try to gauge whether the package is heavier than it was before, and if it is, whether we can cut it with anything that will salvage its appearance, so we can sell it, and if we can't, where the fuck we're going to find the money from to pay the Scousers. And what am I going to tell Lydia?! I imagine all the ways they could kill me – or, worse, *silence me* – and then imagine doing it to Dom – it's the only thing that will keep my head clear.

James

The banging on the glass doors jolts me awake. Who the fuck is here?! And how did they get here? I would have heard a car pulling up on the gravel – my bedroom window looks out over the drive.

Tim stirs but doesn't wake – he was absolutely wasted last night. I creep out of bed and tiptoe down the stairs, my heart hammering in my chest. I'm about to grab a carving knife from the kitchen when I hear, "Tim! James! For fuck's sake, let me in!" It sounds like Will. I run to the lounge and open the patio doors. Will and some other bloke almost fall in, and stand, dripping wet, on the carpet.

"What …?!"

"Just fucking lock the doors and get us a towel and a beer or something!" Will barks, staring daggers at me. So that's what I do.

Ten minutes later, a hungover, sleepy Tim, a bedraggled Will and the other guy, who transpires to be his schizo brother, Dom, and I are sitting at the kitchen table, swigging from cans of Krony. We swig in silence, because the coke is fucked. No one can believe that I can't just magic it fixed with some chemical that I can just pull out of my ass, it seems. This situation is so far west, I wonder what fucking planet they're all on.

"But you're a chemist!" Tim is saying. "Surely you can get something out of the cupboard at uni that we can cut it up with!"

"It isn't fucking Hogwarts, Tim! And I'm not a fucking wizard!"

"What the fuck are you on about, man?" Will shouts, "We need this sorted! Either we cut it with something and sell it, or we come up with the money for it ourselves!"

"Hang on a minute," Tim says, "what do you mean, 'we come up with the money for it, ourselves'? There's a couple of thousand quid's worth of coke, there! And this is supposed to be making us money, not fucking losing it for us!"

"Look, none of us know what we're doing, so cutting it's not an option. I know they say you can cut it with icing sugar and washing powder and that, but if people realise that we've sold them shady gear, then they won't buy it from us again. And if it gets back to the lads up north, they'll fucking kill us. Also – and I don't know if any of you gobshites have thought about this minor detail – if we cut it, it could fucking kill someone!"

"It's cocaine, man!" Will yells. "You do it at your own risk. Everyone knows that."

"Yeah," says his brother, "that's half the fun of it."

There's another silence. I stare at the table. How the fucking hell did I end up in this mess? Tim's hand slides into my vision, reaching covertly for my leg. I brush it away. I've got to get out of this.

I stand up and fill the kettle with water. I need to wake up. I need to sober up. I slam the kettle onto its base and face the others, who are staring at me.

"We all know what's going to happen, so I'm going to tell you how it's going to happen. I'll get the money – I know that's what you're all thinking. I'll get you the money – even though it's your brother's fucking mess," I spit, staring at Will. "And then I'm out. You can't use this cove or this house. Don't want a bar of any of it. I'm fucking done."

Tim staggers to his feet, and tries to cuddle me, even though it's in front of the others, but I shove him back.

"I mean it, Tim!" I shout at him, but I can hear the wobble in my voice. "I'm fucking done – with all of you! I'm going to go back to Liverpool, I'm going to get my degree, and I never want to see any of you fuckers again!"

Tim

"James! James! You can't do this to me!" I'm smashing my fists into the patio doors of his parents 'place at the top of Horse Cove, but he's turned all the lights off and closed all the curtains. Will's scrawny arms grab me round the waist, and he yanks me away. We end up round the front, on the drive where I abandoned my car on the gravel yesterday because James and I couldn't keep our hands off each other. The memory of it makes me cry out.

"Get a fucking grip, Tim." There's more compassion in Will's tone than anger, and I let him lead me round to the driver's door. His crazy brother is quiet – he must be riddled with guilt. James and I both think that all this is his fault, and I'm surprised Will is sticking up for him so much. But then it's a moot point: Dom's on DLA and lives in a care home – he's got no money. The only way he could get any is by robbing someone – maybe even us – and then he'd do a runner with it. James is right. He's the only one of us who can get his hands on that sort of cash. Unless I took a loan. Or broke a big story and sold it to the nationals. But I'm beginning to realise that the latter is a pipe dream.

My mind swerves between heartbreak over James, fear that the lads from Liverpool will crucify us, and the obvious solution to this problem. As we reach the end of the dark track and slide back onto the main road into Swansburne, I've made my decision. I'll call James in the morning. I'll go to the bank and take a loan first thing on

Monday, and get this debt paid. And then I'll wait for news of the next drop. Me and James can set Will and those Scouse fuckers up, and then get on with our lives. It's collateral damage. But we'll have to get rid of the cottage on Belmont Road, first.

"Pull over." I obey Will instantly and stop the car at the far end of Brunswick Street, opposite the public toilets. "Get out." This is not meant for me, so I watch the brothers in my rear-view mirror. Dom looks daggers at his brother but doesn't argue. He's about to slam the door, when Will says, "Go in the loos and sort yourself out. Then go home." He slides his hand into his sodden denim jacket and pulls out a wrap of notes. He chucks it as far as he can towards the open door. "Get some vodka, or whatever the fuck else you want, but do not contact me again!" I hear Dom reach in and grab the bundle, then I watch him stalk off up the road and disappear into the toilets. Will leans over and slams Dom's door, then gets out himself. He gets in the passenger side and stares at me. "Well? Get us the fuck out of here!"

I pull up in the car park behind The Riverboat, and Will gets out. He doesn't say anything – just gives me a nod and wanders off. I sit in the car and eventually turn off the engine. Now that I have a plan, thinking about it can't distract me from the horror of possibly losing James. Grief floods me. I lean my head on the steering wheel and sob.

"Oi! Timmy-boy!"

Stuart is banging on my window, a rollie jammed in his fist and a pint in his other hand. He's wasted. He grabs the door handle, wrenches it open, and shoves his beery face into my car.

"Cheer up, mate," he says, "it might never happen!"

I'm about to tell him to fuck off when I get a whiff of dope. The rollie isn't a rollie – it's a really crap joint. Stuart clocks me looking at it and says, "Here y'are, mate!" and passes it to me. I take a long pull and he nods at me in approval. I hold the smoke in for as long as I can stand it, then let it slowly out of my nose. "Well, here's a man who's in for a lock-in!" he laughs and whacks me on the back. His face has gone all rubbery, and I can't suppress a laugh.

"Yeah, mate," I say, "you're on."

We walk into the back bar of The Riverboat together. Pissed as he is, Stuart has the presence of mind to close the doors and windows and lock up behind us. The lights in the front bar are off. It's late – everyone is long gone. Stuart lurches round behind the bar and pulls himself another pint. Barney is still here, in his stupid coat, as well as a few of his mates and a gaggle of thin, probably underaged girls, who are shivering in their vest tops.

"Wrack us up a load of Aftershocks, mate!" Barney calls to Stuart, with a wink. "We need to warm these girls up a bit!"

"Tim and I'll have a couple, too, please, when you're ready, Stuart."

I whip round, my smile so wide it feels like my face is going to split. Alex returns it, laughing.

"Hello, stranger!" Alex joins me at the bar and Stuart plonks our Aftershocks down in front of us. I start to stammer out an apology, but Alex cuts me off. "Look, don't worry about it. Toast to winning the Vase?" He raises his glass and waits for me to do the same. "Esky Town for the Football League!"

We down our shots and both involuntarily shudder, which makes us laugh, which breaks any remaining ice. "I saw your byline in the paper," Alex says nervously, "but you weren't in the press box?"

I stare at the floor. "I know. I just … I just couldn't … it would have been awkward. I'm sorry."

"Don't worry about it. We're here now," he smiles. Stuart opens a panel on the jukebox and fiddles around until the opening riff of *Enter Sandman* blasts out and everyone cheers and gets involved with what's happening on the pool table.

Eventually, Alex and I are having a match, and he turns out to be a bigger hustler than me! I fluff a shot and nearly tear the baize, and Stuart says, "Right, lads, it's time to up your game!" and pulls a massive wrap of coke out of his jeans pocket. "Everyone who wants some, chuck in twenty quid!" Notes are thrown on the table, and I step back. I look at Alex to find that his eyes are fixed on mine – not twinkling with excitement but challenging and almost hard. I get the overwhelming sensation that I'm at a crossroads.

"Timmy-boy, you in?" Stuart shouts, raising his head as he grabs all the notes. One of the girls produces a mirror from her handbag and starts cutting up the block with her cash card. With her eyes fixed on her task, I can see all the clumps of mascara in her eyelashes. She must have had some earlier, because she's gurning, and I know that if I kissed her, she'd taste of blood, from where she's bitten her cheeks. Then it hits me that I haven't seen Sally in ages.

I find myself standing next to Alex, saying, "Cheers, Stuart, but I'm going to call it a night – I've got shitloads of stuff to sort out in the morning." But he's got his arm round the girl's waist, stroking her side as she snorts a line through a tenner, and winks at me.

Alex draws the bolt back and the black gates crack open. He pushes them closed, but it's only for appearances – town is dead now. We both turn left.

"Oh, are you staying …" Alex trails off.

"My car's in the car park." I pause. "How come you're in Esky, anyway?"

"Oh, I'm staying with a mate in Farefield …" He trails off again. It's the first time he's ever bullshitted me. "Look, Tim. There's something I need to talk to you about. I don't want to make this awkward, but … do you want to come back to mine for a coffee?"

Fogged by alcohol and conflicting emotions, I walk with

Alex down Thomas Street, letting my vision blur so I can make amber jewels from the glow of the streetlights in the puddles. Halfway down the street, he grabs my arm and pulls me to the left, into the front yard of number ten. We stumble together to the door, and just when I think he is going to push me up against it and kiss me, he pulls a key out of his pocket and whispers, "Here we are. Home sweet home."

I'm too surprised to say anything other than, "What …?", and follow him inside. The house is the same as Will's, just backwards. The cold suggests damp, the entrance hall is dark, and narrow stairways separate the floors. This place has clearly been converted into flats, too, and Alex and I climb to the top floor. It's so dark that Alex has to flip a light on for us to be able to see anything at all. The stairs open on a very small square landing, off which are two doors. Alex unlocks the one dead ahead of us, flips on another light and we step inside.

"Talk about the mad bloke in the attic, eh?!" he says, depositing his keys in a little dish on the telephone table. I smile, but I'm on edge. The space is almost square, and the only natural light comes from a small window set into and projecting out from the apex of the roof. The glow from the streetlights makes an orange stain across the floorboards to our feet. Underneath it are a pair of stepladders, opened up to hold a tool box or something. The window is curtainless, so I presume Alex's putting one up. On the left is a row of cupboards that look like they've been reclaimed from Ashley tip; on top of them stand a plastic travel kettle, a camping stove, a couple of pans and a mug tree which holds three mismatched mugs. On the other side of the room is a low, battered Chesterfield sofa. Alex heads for it, stooping before he sits, to allow for the slope of the roof. He stretches out his long legs under a huge wooden coffee table. On it are a ghetto blaster straight out of the eighties, and one of the little Toshiba TVs that Mum and Dad got for me and Cath to have in our rooms. Alex motions for me to sit down and pulls a couple of bottles of Bud out of the mini fridge down by the side of the sofa. He's already got a bottle opener in his hand.

I don't say anything, but perch on the edge of the sofa out of arm's reach of him, waiting for him to explain, but I take the Bud he's holding out for me, and stare at the ladders.

It's not tools that they're holding, but notebooks, pens, a camera, rolls of film and a pair of binoculars. I flip my gaze back to Alex, who shunts forwards in his seat, places his bottle on the table, and takes a deep breath.

"Do you remember the day we met?" he asks, quietly.

"Yeah. At the football." I'm on my guard and my tone is cold.

"Fucking hell, Tim," he says. "I don't want to launch into a monologue, so I'll do a Terry Cooper, and just get on with it. Basically, I clapped eyes on you, and I saw a younger me. Don't look away – I know how it sounds, but that's the whole thing about cliches! A few years ago, I was like you: a young, confused man in a shithole of a town, still in the closet, still shagging girls and trying to lose myself in my work and alcohol to deal with it. I had a part-time job on the local rag, was on antidepressants, and some days it was hard not to just shove the whole lot in my mouth and be done with it.

"Then I met this girl. She'd come down from head office in Liverpool to train us all up on the new computer system – Tera. She was so confident and together and vibrant, and I just thought, *if I could get with her, she could be my way out of here.*

"So I started flirting with her, then I took her out for a drink, and the next thing I knew, I'd been offered a position on the *Liverpool Echo*, and I moved up with her. She had this penthouse apartment, she drove an Audi, she was doing well for herself, and suddenly I was as well. Then one day she took me to a party at this place on Regent Road. It was fucking mental. Everyone was doing drugs there – all kinds of things – acid, K, MDMA, and of course, coke. That was her thing. I tried it a few times, but I just felt really anxious and paranoid about the police, so I stuck to smoking a bit of weed instead. In the end I gave that up, though, because it made me really tired and my brain all foggy, and I had to be on the ball for work – a city daily and a weekly local rag are at opposite ends of the spectrum; but if your objectives are to lose yourself in your work and make a wage that will set you free, then you have to expect to work hard. You have to keep yourself sharp.

"Everything was working for me – I had a job I loved, a beautiful girlfriend, and we were raking it in. Also, she was out a lot after work with the girls in IT. They went clubbing, and she'd turn up in the early hours of the morning, fall into bed, snort a couple of lines in the morning, and do it all again. But she was brilliant at her job – she really was – and because she was out so much, it meant that we didn't have sex very often, which suited me perfectly, obviously. I felt bad, though, because I was … well … I was using her ... so when she started going a bit weird, I just kind of put up with it. She'd get really irritable, and she was losing loads of weight; she stopped cooking – she was a great cook – and then suddenly I was paying all the bills and everything, but I thought, *nothing's ever perfect* and just got on with it.

"Then one night she came home totally off her face – I mean, really gone. She was paranoid, ranting about how everyone was out to get her – myself included – that no one had ever loved her, and she had the razor she used to cut her lines with because she always said that using bank cards was vulgar, and she was waving it around, and then she slashed her wrists, right in front of me. I mean, Jesus, the blood! Fucking hell, there was so much of it, and it was spurting because she'd gone so deep, and when the ambulance came, I was left to clear it all up. There were pools of it in the grouting and on the draining board, and it clots so quickly, it was like … like oil and tar and treacle … like Marmite, almost. And if I knocked a deep pool of it, the skin on it would wrinkle but it would be wobbly underneath – fucking hell, I've never told anyone any of this – fuck, sorry, I'm crying … Jesus, Tim, are you okay?!"

Alex scrambles over the sofa to me, but I can hardly make out his expression because a deluge is coming out of my eyes, and I can't get my breath. I try to bat him away, but all I do is drop my bottle of Bud – I can hear my throat tearing itself to let air in, but none's getting through, and I feel so weak and I'm ripping my clothes away from my throat …

Alex and I are sitting on the floor. Our legs are stretched out in front of us, his outside mine. My back rests against his chest. I can feel his lungs inflating and deflating, slowly and fully, and find my own are mimicking his. Suddenly exhausted, I let my head drop onto his left shoulder, and he leans his into mine. We sit like that for a long time, just breathing together.

"I'm so sorry about your sister, Tim." Alex's voice cracks, and I feel his tears drip onto my bare shoulder. "I had no idea. I … I don't even know what to say … I'm just … sorry."

"Don't worry about it. It's not your fault. I think we could probably both use some counselling!" I try to make my voice bright, but I'm so tired. I don't want to talk, but we can't sit in silence, so I say, "So what happened? To your girlfriend? Did she die?"

"No. Thankfully, no, she didn't. But she got sectioned for a while. Then one day I went to fill up my car so I could visit her in hospital – you know, when she was allowed visitors – and my card was declined. I tried to get some cash out, but she'd drained me. She'd spent the whole fucking lot on drugs. But I couldn't hate her because I'd been using her, too. So I just had to get on with things. And all I could think of was that if I broke a big story, I could sell it to the nationals and make my money back. And hopefully get some dealers off the streets, too. I didn't know how it would work with the police, but all I had was my job, so … Yeah – I know it was fucking naïve!

"Anyway, she wouldn't tell me anything. They moved her to this care home down in Bishopsham because there were no spaces in any of the psych units in Liverpool, and she just clammed up about it. And that's how I ended up down here – you always said people don't choose to live here; they're either born here or end up here through a series of horrendous events! She got better, but either they really didn't want me to see her, or she was making that up because she really didn't want to see me, and one day we just had this fucking hideous argument, and she called me a user and a liar and that she knew I was gay; that's why she'd done so much coke – to escape it. Basically, she blamed everything on me. Fucking bitch.

"Anyway, because we'd been engaged – shit, did I not mention that? – and she was pretty much estranged from her family, the psych services said I was her 'nearest relative'. So when they thought she was well enough to be trusted, they let her go out for walks, and they discussed this with me, but she still wouldn't see me, so one day I went up and – well, I basically spied on the place, waiting for her to come out and go for a walk, so I could confront her. But when she did, I just kind of knew there was something up – like a gut instinct or something – she looked so sad and deflated – so I followed her. She met up with this bloke, and they did the funny handshake. I knew she was involved with drugs again. And I felt sorry for her. So I thought I could kill two birds with one stone – I'd get a good story that I could sell, and I'd stop wankers like that preying on nice girls like her. And I asked one of my mates

– well, contacts, really – in the police what I should do, and I kind of became an informer, but I said I'd only do it if they gave me exclusive rights to the story and let me sell it. The bloke just laughed in my face and said that if I thought I was going to bring down a cartel by watching some small-time dealer, I was fucking delusional, and that the only part of the story a national newspaper would pay for is the bit about me being so soft. Then he said that if I didn't grass on my girlfriend, he'd do me for perverting the course of justice. Please don't look at me like that!

"Anyway, she'd met the bloke by this B & B down near the station, and she met him there a few times. I tried to get photos, but it wasn't really happening, so I decided to rent a room in the flats opposite and watch them. Once my money had gone in from the Echo, I quit my job – I know, it seems like I'm the psychotic one! – but I kind of got fixed on trying to rid the world of evil fuckers who make life a misery for people who are just trying to do their best. I topped up my money by freelancing – you know, with the football reports.

"And then one day, she went into the B & B with this shopping bag, and the next thing I know, she's in the room on the top floor cutting herself up and trying to fix a noose to the light fitting. So I ran in and got the owners and bashed the fucking door down, and saved her life. But I had to pretend I was getting off on watching people in that room – like I was a perverted voyeur. It was a fucking nightmare. But I'd seen enough of the bloke she'd been meeting, and I was just so fucking angry that he'd ruined her life and then ruined mine, and I felt so guilty about Elle –"

"Elle? That was your girlfriend's name? Elle?"

"Yeah, I didn't realise it was just her nickname because she was always 'Elle 'in her bylines, but that's beside the point – I guess I projected it all on to him, so I followed him. Fuck, one night I got pissed and tried to shoot him with a pellet gun! Yeah, so I followed him and," Alex points to the ladders, "I'm still following him now."

I'm speechless and my eyes are watering. I already know the answer, but I ask the question anyway, "Alex – what was your girlfriend's real name?"

"Lydia."

Richard

The best thing about this little arrangement with Kayleigh is Adam's nightshifts. Although her mum is around a fair bit in the day, she religiously goes 'home 'to the cottage she's renting on Belmont Road once Liam is settled in bed at about half six. I know this because I've been watching the house. The thing with Eskwich is that it is full of weirdos and doleites and spastics who sit for hours on the myriad memorial benches that pepper the streets, staring into space – no one bats an eyelid at a bloke in a tracksuit sitting under the beech tree in the church grounds, chain-smoking, especially if they're wearing an anorak and are sitting on a wall, swinging their legs. It means that although Kayleigh has a job, a mother, a young son, friends and a live-in shag, I've still managed to find plenty of time for us to be together.

She is completely – although not blissfully – unaware that Adam has lost his job, and that he spends his 'twelve-hour nightshifts 'dossing in a drugs den so he won't have to admit to her that he can't support his wife and kid. All I have to do is sit and smoke and watch him slope off in his Farefield Fabrics T-shirt at ten to six, wait for her mother to flounce out at just after six-thirty, and then throw a beech nut or a stone at her front room window. She can't refuse to let me in – I have too much over her. All she can do is lie back and think of England and keep her stupid hippy mouth shut. To be fair, I do more of the lying back than she does, and her mouth is often open as wide as it can go.

The best thing about it is, she's supremely willing to drink all the wine, or take a few extra tablets for me – I know it helps her to disassociate. This means I can then have some peace and quiet, and can listen to her loser of a landlord, Will, arrange his drug deals with his little twatty friends on the mobile phone he thinks is his secret; that, or listen to him argue with someone who may or may not be called 'Dom', who persists on calling Will on the phone in the hall. It's amazing what you can overhear when people think that their neighbours are asleep, or out, or working nights. It's amazing what you can do when you learn to be quiet and focus your anger. I am great at playing the long game. And it's amazing that people persist in leaving their private letters in the same hiding place, even when their house has been broken into before – it looks like poor Kayleigh is having trouble with her mental health again. Oh, boo hoo hoo.

Will

I can't believe I'm actually doing this. I am in the front room, hiding behind the curtain at the side of the bay window, wondering how effective net curtains are. He's watching me – the perv in the top flat opposite – not just Kayleigh. At first it was a gut feeling, because whenever I got back home from a pick-up, no matter what time of night it was, I could see that a sidelight was on in his attic room, and as soon as I stepped inside my front door, I'd hear him bang his window closed. Like all the windows in these Victorian terraces, the wooden frames expand when it's wet, and you have to yank them a few times to get them to close, or really shove them to get them to open, and because it rains so much down here, you get so used to being violent with them that when it's actually been sunny and hot for a bit, you end up slamming them shut and then the single pane of glass rattles.

Admittedly, I did wonder if it was the coke making me paranoid, but since things started getting serious, I've stopped doing it; anyway, I can almost feel him watching me. When I'm in Kayleigh's flat, I can see the binoculars and the camera on his windowsill. I wonder what photos he's got of Kayleigh; I get turned on just at the thought of it. But then I've actually shagged her, so he can fuck off. Unless he gets off on the chase. I don't know how she hasn't noticed. Maybe she has.

Anyway, he knows what we look like and what we do, so now I'm going to find out what he looks like and what he does. Except I can't stand behind the curtains all day – I've only been here quarter of an hour, and my back's already aching. And I need a cigarette. As soon as I've had the thought, the craving gets me so bad, that I leave my post, pull out my baccy and go outside. I spark it up, look right up at his attic window, and flick him the Vs. I've no idea if he's even there.

I drop the butt into the flowerpot and immediately roll another. I need the headrush to take the edge off. It's my day off, and I need to put petrol in the van, clear up a bit, and get some food in. I've been living off KFC, Bourbon biscuits, and cigarettes for I don't know how long, and when I went to make a coffee this morning, the milk had turned to cottage cheese in its container. It's a perfect day to get some washing out on the line, as Mum would say. I've been in these jeans for days, and there's a brown tidemark up to my ankles. The jeans are frayed to fuck, too – I ought to get some new clothes.

"Morning, Will!" It's Kayleigh's mum, Sandra. She's pushing a sleeping Liam in his buggy. I wonder where Kayleigh is. "Mind if I join you?" She stands a couple of feet away, pulls a Silk Cut out of the packet that's sticking out of her open handbag, and offers the packet to me. "Well, it's almost afternoon, actually," she giggles, checking her gold chain watch. I thank her and take one. It would be rude not to. I go to spark mine up, but my lighter's nearly out of gas, and it just clicks. I give it a shake and try again, and then Kayleigh's mum steps towards me in a cloud of heady perfume, and lights it for me with her gold Zippo. In that moment, she's too close to me, and I try to step back, but bump my head on the drainpipe. She steps away, embarrassed, and I feel myself blush. We both sort of chuckle, and she flicks her eyes to meet mine, several times. I take a long drag and fix my gaze on the crows strutting about on the grass in the church yard. The leaves have just started to turn, and when it's quiet, you can hear the first beech nuts dropping on the pathway.

"Will …" And now I have to look at her again, and my cheeks burn. I have no idea why I'm blushing. Fucking hell, maybe I have done too many drugs, and messed up my brain. "It's about Kayleigh," she tries again. "I know you've always had her best interests at heart – you were so good when she got ill and went to hospital that time. Honestly, I don't know what she'd have done without you. Anyway, I thought she was better – I mean Adam came back, and she is great with Liam, and I couldn't believe she'd actually been," she whispers the next word and mouths it exaggeratedly, "*sectioned*. But since we saw on the news that Richard is out, she's been getting worse again. Nothing major, you know, but she's definitely not been *right*."

She's waiting for a response, so I say, "Oh, I'm so sorry to hear that. In what way? Do you think she needs to see someone again?" I'm aware of the perv over the road, so I'm keeping my voice low, but he probably knows anyway.

"Well, that's the thing, Will – she's seeing Dr Whittle again, and they're talking about hospital." She stares me right in the face. I remember the night I made the call that got Kayleigh sectioned in the first place. I remember her face in the back of the car, pale and flecked with blood, crying into Liam's T-rex toy. I can never, never tell them that it was me who made the call.

Sandra interrupts the memory. "Oh, look, Will," she says, flicking a column of ash off the end of her cigarette, "I may as well be completely honest with you. Would you mind coming inside for a moment?"

We finish our cigarettes in a couple of puffs – straights just burn away; it's a waste, really – stub them out in the plant pots, and go inside. I close the door as quietly as I can, so as not to wake Liam, then push in front of Sandra so that I can grab the front of the buggy and help her carry him upstairs. We go slowly – it's awkward as the stairs are so narrow, and there's very little grip on the threadbare blue carpet. I bash my elbow on the wall as we turn the corner up to Kayleigh's flat.

Once inside, Sandra wheels Liam into the front room – he hasn't even stirred – then I follow her into the kitchen, where she makes a coffee. She hands me the Ugly Mug that Kayleigh always gives me, realises what she's done, and apologises with a laugh – apparently, it's the only clean one – rinses a Groovy Chick one out for herself, and then apologises for the state of the kitchen.

Kayleigh's house has never been the tidiest, but mainly because she has so much stuff, and every flat surface is covered with candles or crystals, or – nowadays – baby paraphernalia, but I've never seen it dirty before. The sink is full of pans and dishes, and there are used mugs all over the worktops. The lid of the bin is encrusted with something dark and sticky looking, and a squashed box of Farley's Rusks has wedged it open. The floor is littered with crumbs and strands of green stuff. It's nowhere near as bad as mine.

In the front room, I sit so I can see the perv's window. I can't see his binoculars. Maybe he wasn't in after all. Before I realise it, I've asked, "Where is Kayleigh, anyway?"

Sandra pushes Liam's T-rex further back into his buggy, and says, "Well, that's just the thing, Will. She is seeing Dr Whittle again. In fact – I can't believe I'm saying this – she's in hospital again." Sandra sobs involuntarily and faffs around in her bag until she finds a pack of tissues. "I'm sorry," she says, dabbing under her eyes. I wonder how old she is. She's not glamorous, like Cath's mum, but she's always well-dressed and made up. I expect she uses Oil of Ulay, like Kayleigh does. She's waiting for a response, again.

"Oh no!" I exclaim, a beat too late. "Is there anything I can do? How long is she going to be in there …?" I trail off because Sandra is clearly itching to tell me all about it. It's like she just needs someone to listen to her. I wonder how much Kayleigh's dad is doing – if he even knows.

"Well, she's actually gone in as a voluntary patient. They call it 'Section 17', and it isn't really voluntary, because if she refuses, they're just going to section her again anyway." Sandra tries to stop her chin from wobbling, but the tears are falling, so she just lets herself cry for a bit. I'm embarrassed, but I go over and sit next to her, and pat her shoulder. She raises her head and smiles at this, and gains control with a bashful laugh. Kayleigh has inherited her hair – the slightest hint of moisture in the air and it fluffs up and curls.

"I'm sorry!" she says, and blows her nose loudly, which makes us both laugh. "Because she's got Liam, she's allowed home either overnight, or for a few hours in the day, and she can come out with me if I go and visit. That's why neither of us has been around much recently."

"What about Adam?" I can't help but ask. "What does he make of it?" I'm surprised he hasn't said anything. But then if he can keep the fact that he's lost his job from Kayleigh, then he can keep the fact that she's been sectioned again from me.

"Well, he gets up and goes to work, takes Liam for a bit in the day, but I'm doing the bulk of the childcare, to be honest. Not that I mind – Liam's my grandson, and he's a wonderful little boy, and Adam has got to work, obviously: someone has to pay the rent! But it's a mess, Will, it really is. I hope you don't mind me being frank with you like this, but you're the only person I can talk to!" A pause. "I'm sorry, that sounds awful – what a back-handed compliment!"

I kind of laugh. "Don't worry about it – I know what you meant! If there's anything I can do, just let me know."

"Of course, thank you, Will. By the way, Kayleigh asked me not to say anything to anyone, so if you do see her, please don't mention anything!" Sandra drains her coffee and places it down hard on the coffee table. It clinks, and she winces, her eye darting to Liam. "He's such a sound sleeper," she says with a sigh. "Kayleigh doesn't realise how lucky she is! But then she did wake him up early this morning – she wanted to spend as much time as possible with him before she had to be back at The Beeches."

"Oh, does she have to be back at a certain time, then?"

"Yes – if she's out in the day, she has to be back by six o'clock; if she's here overnight, she has to be back at nine. If she's late, she'll lose her privilege." Sandra looks as if she's about to cry again.

I finish my coffee and stand. "Right, I'd better go – I've got more dirty crockery than Kayleigh, and I need to get some washing on!"

"Yes, it's a lovely day for drying it on the line," Sandra says, vaguely.

Will

I'm slumped on the sofa, staring through the grubby net curtains, half-heartedly watching for movement from the perv's window. I'm daydreaming about getting in my car and just running for the hills. Or, rather, from them. Sudden silence wakes me from my reverie – Kayleigh has turned her music off. That Gallagher twat's band is just white noise to me now. I hear her door close slowly, like she's trying to be quiet. Liam must be asleep. Just as I'm wondering what she's doing going off and leaving him, I hear a subtle knock on my door, and "Will!" in an exaggerated whisper. I can't help but smile.

"Hi!" Kayleigh's anxiety is evident. She's holding a baby monitor. "Yeah," she says, following my gaze, "I don't like leaving Liam alone, but I had to come and see you. Is it okay if I come in?"

I hadn't realised I'd left her standing on the threshold like stranger, and I feel myself blush. "Yeah, sure, of course, come in. Long time, no see.' "Long time, no see'?!

Kayleigh hesitates and follows me along the hall. Ordinarily, she'd have walked straight in and started making a coffee. I head into the kitchen, silently thanking God that I cleared up the other day, and put the kettle on. Kayleigh stands nervously against the fridge, fiddling with the baby monitor. Initially, I'm surprised it works at this range, but then I suppose that once this was one house, and Liam is probably sleeping in the room directly above us.

Oddly, I'm embarrassed about my mugs. I've never even thought of it before, but I'm suddenly aware that hanging on a battered pine mug tree are six stained specimens that my parents got with petrol station tokens in the late 80s. In the cupboard below are the matching cereal bowls and milk jug – all white with red and black stripes. I cringe.

"Fuck it!" Kayleigh slams the baby monitor down on the worktop, strides over and embraces me. It's an embrace and not a cuddle – there's deep emotion behind it that compels me to reciprocate. Suddenly, we are kissing, and I can't tell if it's one or both of us who are moaning with need. The kitchen floor just isn't appropriate this time, but I can't take her into my bedroom, so I lead the way back down the hall, and we fall onto the sofa.

Normally I'd be stressing about how quick it is, but I can see Kayleigh's blissed out too, so I tell her I love her, and she smiles and murmurs something, and I think she said she loves me too, but I don't make a big thing of it – I just hold her really tightly and try not to sob. We kind of doze off tangled up in each other. I remember a load of crows going over, cawing at each other, and trying to see them through the net curtains; the next thing I remember is that there are raindrops on the window, but I didn't hear any downpour.

Kayleigh's voice reverberates through my body: "I was reading an Oasis biography the other day. Did you know that Liam is actually short for William?"

Her words turn my body to stone. What does she mean?

"It always comes back to you and me, Will. You're the only person I can trust. We may as well just be together."

And just like that, she breaks my heart for the last time. It's shattered. It's beyond repair. This is over.

James

I'm crying in the train toilets. I've been in here ages, and the train is packed, and someone's banging on the door, but I can't go out in tears. There's nowhere to hide. Tim won't stop ringing my phone. It rings and I see his name pop up and I watch it, through the tears, letting the vibration into the core of my being, but I don't pick up. Eventually my voicemail clicks in, and the phone goes silent for a minute, and then he's ringing again. He won't stop. Why is he doing this to me?! He almost ruined my life. I'm going back to Liverpool, I'm concentrating on my degree, I've still got my room in Mulberry Court, I'm going to get my degree and find a cure for cancer and make my parents proud of me. They've forgiven me, but they're disappointed. I can see it in their eyes and it's killing me. The lady tutting on the other side of the door is banging harder, shouting that their kid is bursting. I don't know whether to push my phone out of the grubby little toilet window or flush it down the toilet. I do neither – just switch it off and thrust it into my jeans pocket – storm out of the cubicle, and look the woman straight in the eye. Our expressions swap places.

"I'm so sorry," she says to the back of my head.

"Excuse me," says a man's voice, "I think your little boy

has had an accident."

Tim

Alex says he loves me. Alex says we can set them up, together. Alex says he'll split the money with me – or we can use it to be together. Alex says we'll be doing the world a favour. Alex says we're the same.

Alex is right – in the most part. But he's not sharp.

Alex doesn't come from round here. Alex doesn't know that people get Horse Cove and Shell Cove muddled up all the time.

Alex doesn't know that I love James.

James

I can't believe I'm making this journey again so soon. The train is packed. I'd booked a seat with a table so that I could work on the way down, but I'm too shaky to concentrate. Partly it's because I have a couple of thousand quid in notes on my person, partly it's because I'm still reeling from telling my parents everything. I've been staring out of the window since I sat down, and I've got my headphones in and my portable CD player on the table. I can't make it any more obvious that I don't want to talk, but I can feel the girl opposite staring at me. The train starts up, and we crawl out of Lime Street; by the time the urban sprawl turns to open countryside, she's given up on me, and is talking to the bloke in the suit who's in the seat next to her. I can't make out what it says on the orange and white reservation ticket stuck in the top of her seat, but she's got a Brummie accent, so I bet she'll be there until we change at Birmingham New Street. I turn my music up.

By the time we leave Bristol, I'm having trouble keeping my eyes open. There's hardly anyone in my carriage now, thank goodness, so I rest my feet on the seat that the annoying girl was sitting in, and lean back as far as I can in my seat. Feeling safe that no one's going to try to make conversation, I take my headphones out. They've been hurting my ears for the last two hours. My eyes close, but I can't risk falling asleep, so I get my little travel alarm clock out. I've had it for years. It's just a white plastic square thing, but I love it because it doesn't tick. I put it on the table in front of me, set the alarm for half an hour, pat the clock on its 'head', and berate myself for being so soft.

But it's not the alarm that wakes me – it's my mobile phone. The irritating ring tone is loud and brash in the quiet carriage; incongruous with the darkness outside and the soft rhythm of the train on its rails. I pick it up, intending to switch it off, but I'm worried it's Will, calling about our little rendezvous, so I answer before I've recognised the number as Tim's.

I don't say anything.

"James, this isn't about us. It's about you and Will meeting later." His voice is cracking, but he sounds scared, and instinct tells me to listen.

I'm opening the carriage door the second the train stops, then I hurry out of St Davids station. It's a real effort not to run, but I ignore the length of the platforms and the seemingly endless stairs and keep my eyes on the signs. I bet this place is pretty when you're not running scared. When I leave the main entrance, I expect the drop-off area to be full of police cars, but it's not. Will won't be in his Polo, he will be in the taxi that's waiting at the bus stop. I jog up to it, glance in the passenger-side window, meet his steely gaze and jump in the back with my rucksack at his nod. I'm surprised when he says, "All right, Rob?" and mutter back a "Yeah."

"Brizzol uni treating you well?"

"Yeah."

"Tired?"

"Yeah, sorry, haha!" I try to flatten the Scouse out of my accent, then pretend to fall asleep in the back, while Will chats to the driver.

I don't wake up until he shouts "Rob!" and I grab my stuff, stumble out of the back of the cab and find we've pulled over on the side of a through-road, outside a pub called Malloy's. "Where is it?" he says under his breath. He means the money.

"It's in my jacket," I say. I have no idea what's going on, so I follow Will into the pub and prop myself up at the bar.

"I'll get these," Will says, smiling, and gestures the lad behind the bar over. "Two pints of Krony, please, mate," he says. "Bloody hot in here, innit?!" He takes off his battered denim jacket, and I do the same. The beers come, and he takes a swig. "I'm going for a slash," he says, and then he's gone. It's not till I look for the pouch of baccy I had in my pocket that I realise he's taken my jacket and left me with his.

He's gone for ages, but I try to look normal, and work out where we are. I drink my pint slowly and cadge a cigarette off a girl who lurches over and tries to chat me up. She smells of cider, vanilla, and weed, and wants to *get out of Tamehaven*. So that's where we are. I wonder if there's anyone in the entire world who doesn't want to get out of the town they grew up in.

It's getting on for last orders when Will reappears, and he looks as exhausted as I feel. The girl has fallen asleep with her head on the beer barrel tables, so I down the dregs of my pint and follow him out to his car, which is parked on the opposite side of the road outside a big house bearing the name Tame View.

"It's done," he says, without looking at me. "Now we have to grab what's been dropped and lose that fucking boat. I take it you cleaned the house up after you chucked us out and left?"

"Yeah, of course! It's my fucking parents 'house!"

"No Rizlas? No powder on the CDs?"

"Don't be a fucking twat, Will, I wasn't born yesterday!

And if it hadn't been for you and your dick of a brother, there would never have been any coke in there anyway!"

"No empty bottles? No dirty ashtrays? No dirty sheets …?"

"Fuck off."

"No mugs in the dishwasher? No milk in the fridge?"

"No! Oh, hang on, yeah, there's milk, because I made myself a coffee before I left. I rinsed the mug out and put it back in the cupboard, though. What's the big deal?"

"It's supposed to be a holiday home that hasn't been used yet, you fucking idiot!"

"I'll just say Tim and I stayed there."

"What? When he's got a flat in Eskwich, and no one's seen you out in Swansburne, or sunbathing on the beach, even?"

"It's just milk!"

"Yeah – milk that has a fucking sell-by date on it!"

Will speeds up the lane to my parents 'holiday home and crunches to a stop on the gravel. "Gravel?!" he hisses. I jump out, fumbling with the keys, and when I'm inside, I run straight to the fridge and grab the milk. I have my sleeve pulled over my hand, and I hope that's enough.

Will joins me at the steps down the cliff – it'll take two of us to drag it up and into the car. If it even fits.

Adam

I'm waiting in a cubicle in A&E. I can hear voices from the nurses 'station – "… I know, but they know she's poorly, yeah? I mean you've got to have that conversation with them … I know it's hard and I do feel for you, but they need to be given a chance to say 'goodbye' …"

They're talking about Kayleigh's folks, I know they are. Why would I count? I'm only the boyfriend. I'm only the father of her child! This 'family room 'is too warm, and the air is thick with the stench of cold coffee and stale sweat. I concentrate on the sounds of life coming from outside –

voices, beeps, the squeak of trainers on newly disinfected floors, nervous laughter, and the occasional clink of coffee mugs.

An ache in my back makes me realise that I'm perched on the edge of the settee and am tense as fuck. In the attempt to relax, I flop back into the squishy cushions. The fabric is yellow and threadbare and stained with drops of what I hope is coffee. I'm surprised they let a room in a hospital get this gross, but I suppose they want it to feel a bit homely. Faded fabric flowers in a little plastic pot on the windowsill. Wishy-washy watercolours of what someone thinks is typical country life, in tacky frames. Out-of-date women's magazines. A small plastic storage box with a few battered stacking rings and wooden trains for the kids. Kayleigh's mum, Sandra, will be here with Liam in a minute – she said she'd come over and babysit while Kayleigh went for her appointment with the psychiatrist, because I would have just got home from a twelve-hour night shift in the factory. In fact, I would have just got home from an all-nighter with the lads – I can't bring myself to tell Kayleigh and her mum that I lost my job ages ago – so I stay out drinking or smoking and playing computer games, usually all of the above, round a mate's all night – there's nothing else to do in this shithole of a town – and then do some coke as the sun's coming up to sober me up a bit before I go home. I vaguely remember Kayleigh saying she was off, but I just pulled the duvet over my head and tried to fall asleep before I pulled another whitey. My mouth is stale and rank – I didn't have time to brush my teeth or shower or anything – I just got up and threw yesterday's clothes on when Will hammered on the door and said there was someone on the phone for me. And then I just jumped in Will's car and left. I know I shouldn't have driven, but what the fuck do you do when the hospital phones and tells you your girlfriend has been stabbed?

And now here I am, perched on the edge of this

disgusting old settee, with my head in my hands, dreading Sandra turning up with Liam, and dreading the doctors coming in and telling us that Kayleigh is dead. Someone stabbed her and a load of other people, outside the bloody psych unit! They stabbed her in the neck!

Shit – if she dies, what the fuck am I supposed to do about Liam?!

Will

Oh, how the mighty have fallen! I keep telling people that if you're dealing, you shouldn't be partaking! The critically acclaimed Charcot, playing in The Coal Mine again! And that dick, Rob, wants some coke for the after-party! I can feel it all falling apart. Tim and James have gone, Lydia's in a fucking psych unit, Adam's dad has got wind of things and wants him to work in his bike shop, and I'm still running around after Kayleigh! I need to get rid of this last lot, make a nice amount of cash, and then do a fucking runner, and start again. Leave this shithole of a county behind. I'll go to London, like half of the rest of the world. I'll teach graphic design. No, fuck it, I'll teach art, with a capital 'A'. Dom and Kayleigh are just sponges. Parasites. In survival of the fittest, Dom and Kayleigh and all their kind wouldn't have made it. I need to do something. They've fucked with me, I'll fuck with them. I need some closure. I need some catharsis. I'm so fucking angry, I could die. I'm so fucking angry, I could k-

And when the pupil is ready, the teacher appears! Or something like that. I read this book once, about the law of attraction, or something. Basically, if you visualise something, or take little steps to make it happen, or *will* it to happen, even – it will.

Dom is at the gig. Dom comes back to Rob's flat. Dom is fucked. Kayleigh will be at The Beeches at nine in the morning. It's someone's birthday, and there's a knife in the cake. One in, one out, they say. All I need is something to cover my red hair. They're collateral damage. It's survival of the fittest. Their deaths mean I will flourish and make something of my life and help other people – other people who are actually going to be of some use to society.

It's so easy. I tell Dom to walk into The Beeches and find the girl he loves – the goth girl I saw on the beach that day – and do whatever it takes to get her back, her and their baby. But I know she's not there, because Lydia's told me that Lizzie is in A and E and that she's lost the baby. It's sad, but they say mental illness is hereditary. I'm doing the world a favour.

I wait behind the Jag that's parked up in front of the psych unit. The bloke who got out must be a doctor or something – he was in a suit and had an ID tag. And here comes Kayleigh. She's so pretty and I love her so much and I have done for so long. And I know she loves me. But they say that if you love somebody, you should let them go – and that's what I say to Kayleigh when I put the knife into her pretty, pretty throat. Other people are round me, screaming, so I jab them with the knife, and run for it. They are collateral damage. Then I walk straight to St Davids and buy a packet of sandwiches and an overpriced coffee, sit in the station cafe and wait for my train to London.

"Mr Whiley? Would you like to come in? We've been through your CV, and your portfolio, actually, and I must say, we're greatly impressed! The way you've merged those parrots into the design – well, it's almost trompe l'oeil!"

"Thank you! I was inspired by my brother …"

James

"Hello, mate." I slap Andy on the back, and we end up in one of those necessary but slightly awkward man-embraces.

"Good to see, you, JT. It's been a long time." Andy

smiles, and I can see my best mate again, through all the muscle and facial hair. "Fancy a beer?" He pulls a six-pack out of his rucksack.

"Yeah, thanks, why not?! Oh, and I've got something to remind us of old times." I pull a fat, but slightly crushed, spliff out of my jeans pocket.

"Haha, seriously, mate, I thought you jacked all that in." Andy flops down next to me, and we lean our heads and shoulders against the back of the church. The sun's going down, and it's blissfully warm on my face. I open my eyes to the now hazy sky, that's fading from yellow, through green and to blue, and spot a star to the left of the cathedral, which is just shadow.

"I think that of all the buildings in Liverpool, my favourite is Paddy's Wigwam," Andy says.

"Bloody hell, mate, has that hit you already?!"

"Yeah, but look at it! Look. That cloud could be a fucking smoke signal coming out the top of it, or something!"

"Jesus, Andy, pass it over! You're out of practice!"

"Whatever. Where did you get that shit from anyway? It's fucking A!"

"Oh, you know, it's all over Liverpool." I allow my mind to fall back on the cushion of weed. "You know, if you're not stupid with it, smoking this will help with your leg."

"Yeah. I might get lung cancer and psychosis and lose my memory, but at least I'll be able to play football again!" Andy absentmindedly rubs the leg that some wanker in his old school deliberately broke. Then he says, "Have you got any more?"

"Nah, mate. I've got my viva in the morning. This is a celebratory thing. You know, saying goodbye to the old James …"

"And off to boldly go where – oh fuck it, I can't remember! Here's to new frontiers!" Andy takes a swig of his Krony, and takes a long drag on the spliff, before passing it back. I do the same.

"I fucking love cannabis, mate," I find myself saying. "It's the most underrated drug in the world."

Richard

I'll admit it – I'm smug. For the first time in my life, I feel proud of myself. I keep reading over the documents from UCAS. My top two choices, Liverpool and Manchester, have offered me places starting in October. I finished my coffee ages ago, and I've chain-smoked three Marlboros. I feel like I ought to mark the occasion, but the only alcohol I have in the house is half a bottle of Mad Dog that I opened months ago. My back is against the radiator in the front room, but I've got the sash window up because of the cigarettes, so I'm hot and cold at the same time. Farefield Factory's day shift has just knocked off – I can hear them all piling into The Riverboat and The Stars. There are a load of teenaged girls hanging around the bench on the triangle just up the road – I can hear them giggling and whooping and mock telling each other to fuck off. I can imagine what they're wearing, and what they're not wearing. Years ago, I would have just sauntered up there with my bottle of Mad Dog, and let nature take its course, but tonight I can't muster the enthusiasm. I want something more meaningful. Liverpool or Manchester? I thought I'd go straight for Manchester because that's where Cath was off to before she topped herself and landed me in the shit; but I know Stuart and Will are getting their drugs from Liverpool, and the connection might come in handy. We've all got to make a living, and I saw something on the news about the Tories doing away with student loans. And they've closed down the Hacienda, the bastards. And Liverpool is nearer to the sea, so if I was going to find anything fossil-wise just randomly, I'd be more likely to there.

I unscrew the top of the Mad Dog and sniff it. I don't

know why – this stuff is basically just chemicals and it'll never go off. It's probably got a longer half-life than uranium. I take a swig. It's rank. I stand and look out of the window. People are walking down over the bridge to The Riverboat in droves now. I decide to join them. I can get a drink worthy of the occasion, as well as some coke off Stuart.

Talk of the devil. Here he comes, strutting down past the town hall in his Levi's and Reebok Classics, with his arm round some skinny Baby Spice wannabe. Ha! He's such a twat, splashing his cash and acting like a fucking rock star. And he speaks far too loudly. What a wanker. It's probably all the coke he's doing.

"Nah, Tim's long gone. He fucked off to Liverpool to chase after his bum-chum – yeah! I didn't see that one coming, either! Mind you, neither did Sally. I feel sorry for her. Apparently she's popping Prozac now – talk about ironic …" And him and his bit of fluff break into a rendition of the Alanis Morissette song, before he launches into the argument that he thinks makes him look clever – about how the song, *Ironic,* is actually ironic because all the things she says are ironic are not ironic, they're just Sod's Law. What a loser. I've got to get out of here. And now, I can!

I smile so wide that it feels like my face is going to split, but I'm so happy, I don't care. Cath's brother, Tim, is in Liverpool. Liverpool it is, then! I have a month to get things in order, and then I'm off to take my degree in archaeology, and then palaeontology. If that's not ironic, I don't know what is!

As I stride down to the pub, I notice two seagulls on the bridge railings. One's on one side of the road, facing south, down to Exeter; the other's on the other side, facing north towards the whole of the rest of the country. I charge down the middle of the road, and they both fly off and wheel into the sky. They could shit on all of us.

I love birds. They're the nearest thing we've got to the dinosaurs. When I look in a gull's eye, I can see its inner velociraptor. It's always hunting, always protecting. It's a survivor, like me. Gulls are sickeningly underrated.